MW00584451

Four Novellas of Fear

CORNELL WOOLRICH

A. J. Cornell Publications
New York

"For information" address:
A. J. Cornell Publications
18-74 Corporal Kennedy St.
Bayside, NY 11360

Library of Congress Control Number: 2010900032

ISBN: 978-0-9727439-8-3

Printed in the Unites States of America

CONTENTS

EYES THAT WATCH YOU

The house was a pleasant two-story suburban set in its own plot of ground, not close enough to its neighbors to impair privacy and seclusion, but not far enough away to be lonely or isolated. You could catch glimpses of them all around it through the trees and over the tops of the hedges that separated the lawns. You couldn't command a full view of any of them, and they couldn't command a full view of the house, either.

It had a back porch and a front one, and it had rambler roses trained around the porch posts both in front and in back.

It was midafternoon and Mrs. Janet Miller was sitting in her chair on the back porch. That was because the back of the house faced west and got the afternoon sun. Mornings she sat on the front porch, afternoons on the back. Life had long ago been reduced to its barest essentials for her. The feel of the warm sun on her, the sight of the blue sky over her, the sound of Vern Miller's voice in her ears—those were the only things it held any more, those were the only things left to her. She didn't ask for more, so long as those weren't taken from her as everything else had been.

She sat there uncomplaining, content, almost—yes, almost happy, in her rubber-tired wheelchair, a blanket tucked snugly about her feet and lap. She could feel the sun on her, she could see the sky out through the porch posts, and as for the sound of his voice, that would come a little later—it was too early for that yet. She had that much more to look forward to, at least.

She was sixty, with a pink-cheeked, unlined face, snow-white hair, trustful pottery-blue eyes. She was completely, hopelessly paralyzed from head to foot, had been for the past ten years.

It seemed long ago, another lifetime ago now, that she had last walked on floors, moved up and down stairs, raised her hands to her hair to brush it, to her face to wash it, to her mouth to feed it, or expressed the thoughts that were still as clear, as undimmed as ever in her mind, by the sound of words issuing from her mouth. All that was gone now, gone and unlamented. She had trained herself, forced herself, steeled herself, not to lament it.

No one would ever know what it had cost her to accomplish that much, no one would ever know the private purgatory she had been through, the Via Dolorosa she had traversed. But she had emerged now, she had won her battle. She held tight to what remained to her. No monster-god ever worshipped by the most benighted savages could be cruel enough to take that pitiful remainder from her. The sun, the sky, Vern's voice, remained. She had achieved resignation, acceptance, content. So she sat there motionless in the slanting sun, behind the twining rambler-rose tendrils. Something human, something living, that wanted its happiness too.

The doorbell rang around on the other side of the house, and the footsteps of Vera, Vern's wife, started from the floor above to answer it. But quickly, with a rush, as though she had been waiting for this summons, as though she had seen who it was from one of the upper windows. It must be company then, and not just a tradesman or peddler.

Janet Miller could hear the front door open, then quickly close again, from where she sat. But no gush of feminine salutations followed. Instead a man's voice said, cautiously muted, but not too muted to carry to the sharp ears whose sensitivity had increased rather than diminished since the loss of other faculties: "You alone?"

And Vera's voice answered: "Yes. Did anyone see you come in?"

That first, husky, guarded voice hadn't been *the* voice, hadn't been Vern's. It couldn't be this early—not for another hour or more yet. Who could it be then? A man—that meant it was a friend of Vern's, of course. She knew all his friends and tried to place this one, but couldn't. They never came at this hour. They were all busy downtown, as Vern was himself.

Well, she'd know in a minute. One thing about Vern's friends, the first thing they all did was come and say hello to her, ask her how she was, usually bring her something, some little trifle or dainty. Vera would bring him out with her to see her, or else wheel her in to where he was. She liked to meet company. That wasn't one of the three essentials; that was a little pampering she allowed herself.

But instead of coming through the hall that bisected the house, out to where she was, they turned off into the living-room, and she heard the door close after them, and from then on there wasn't another sound.

She couldn't understand that. Vera had never closed the door like that when they had company before. It must have been just absentmindedness on her part. She'd done it without thinking. Or else maybe it was some little surprise they were preparing, for herself or for Vern, and they wanted to make sure of keeping it a secret. But Vern's birthday was long past, and her own didn't come until February—

She waited patiently but the door stayed closed. It seemed she wasn't to meet this caller, or be wheeled in to him. She sighed a little, disappointedly.

Then suddenly, without warning, they came through into the back of the house, the kitchen. It had a window looking out on the back porch, just a little to one side of where she was seated. She could even see into a very narrow strip of the room by looking out of the far corners of her eyes. She could move her eyes, of course.

Vera came in there first, the caller after her. She seemed to set something down on the kitchen table, then she started to undo it with a great crackling and rattling of paper. Some sort of parcel, evidently. So they were busied about a surprise, a gift, after all.

She heard Vera say, "Where'd you ever get this idea from?" with a sort of admiring, complimentary ring to her voice.

The man answered: "Reading in the papers about how they were passing them out over in London and Paris, when they were scared war was going to break out. Someone I know was over there at the time and brought some of them back with him. I got hold of these from him."

"D'yuh think it'll work?" she asked.

He said: "Well, it's the best idea of the lot we've had so far, isn't it?"

"That doesn't say much for some of the others," Vera answered.

The crackle of unwrapping paper had continued uninterruptedly until now. It stopped at last.

There was a moment's silence, then she said: "Aren't they funny-looking things?"

The man said: "They'll do the trick, though. Never mind how they look."

The paper crackled one last time, then Vera said: "What'd you bring two for?"

"One for the old lady," he answered.

Janet Miller experienced a pleasant little glow of anticipation. They had something for her, they were going to give her something, some little present or memento.

"What for?" she heard Vera say impatiently. "Why not both of them at once?"

"Use your head," the man growled. "That's the one thing we want to avoid. She's our immunity; don't you get it? Sort of like an alibi. As long as nothing happens to her, it's good for an accident. But if they both go then it looks too much like we wanted the decks cleared. Don't let's load the dice against ourselves. One out of three people in a house, we can get away with. But two out of three, and it'll begin to smell fishy. Don't forget you're in the same room with him. She's up at the other end of the hall. How's it going to look if he goes and you, right next to him, don't? And then she goes too, all the way out in another room, with a couple of closed doors in between?"

"All right," Vera conceded grudgingly. "But if you had to push her around all day and wait on her like I do——"

The sunlight falling on Janet Miller seemed to have changed. It was cold, baleful now. She could hear her heart beating, pounding against her ribs, and her breath was coming fast, through fear-distended nostrils.

The man went on: "You better let me show you how to put it on right while I'm here, so you'll know how it goes when the time comes."

Vera started to say something, but her voice was blurred out as though she had stuck her head into a bag.

Suddenly she came too close to the window, moved inadvertently within that narrow segment of the room that the far corners of Janet Miller's eyes could encompass. Her whole head had vanished. If the paralytic had been capable of sound, she would have screamed. Vera had what looked like a horse's feed bag up over her entire face. A nozzle protruded from this and went down somewhere out of sight. Two round gogglelike disks for eyes.

A gas mask!

She shifted further back into the room, out of sight again. Her voice sounded clearly once more. She must have taken it off. "Whew! Stuffy. Are you sure it'll work? I'm not in this to take any chances myself, you know."

"They're made to stand much worse stuff than you're going to get tonight."

"Where'll I keep them? I don't want him to find them before I'm ready for them. I'm afraid if I take them up to the room with me he'll——"

Janet Miller heard the clang of the oven door being opened, pushed closed again. "Here's a place he'll never look into in a million years. Supper's all cooked. I can just warm it on top of the stove. He never bothers with the kitchen much. I'll come down and get them the last thing, after he's asleep. Take the paper out with you."

More crackle of paper, this time being smoothed and folded small, to fit into someone's pocket.

The man's voice said: "That's that. Now have you got everything straight? Put the spare on the old lady. Don't cross me up on that. We're just laying ourselves wide open if you let her go with him. Don't put your own on ahead of time—he's liable to wake up and see you wearing it. Hold out as long as you can before you get into it; it won't hurt you to get a little of the stuff in you. Remember you've got an inhalator squad to buck afterwards.

"Get rid of all the papers and rags stuffed under the windows before they get here. And when you phone the alarm, don't speak over the phone. Your voice is liable to sound too strong. Just knock the receiver off and leave it that way; that'll bring 'em. It'll take a little longer, but what've you got to lose? You're in a fade-out on the floor near the door, just couldn't make it. But the most important thing of all is the masks. If they're found around here afterwards, we're cooked. Take hers and yours off before they get here, when you're sure he's finished, and lock 'em both in the rumble seat of the car, out in the garage. You won't be using it after he's gone. You don't even know how to drive. In a day or two you phone the Ajax Garage—that's my place—to come and get it, take it off your hands, sell it for you. I'll take them out at my end, return them as soon as I can. No one'll ever know the difference."

"How long'll I give him? I've heard of them pulling people through after working over 'em an hour, sometimes more. We want to make sure that don't happen."

"Just see that he soaks up enough, and you can bet all the oxygen in the world won't pull him through. Watch his face. When that gets good and blue, all mottled, you got nothing more to worry about. You better lie low for about a month afterwards. Give them a chance to settle up the estate and all that. I'll give you a ring in—say thirty days from tonight. Are you sure everything's shaped up right?"

"Yeah. He's insured up to his ears. All his stock's been bought in my name. The business has been doing pretty good, and there are no other relatives to horn in. We'll be set for life, Jimmy darling. That's why I held out against doing it any other way but this. There wouldn't've been any sense to it."

"Where's the old lady?" he asked unexpectedly.

"On the back porch where she always is."

"Hey, she can hear us, can't she? Let's get out of here!"

She laughed callously. "Suppose she does? What can she do? Who can she tell? She can't talk, she can't write, she can't even make signs."

They didn't even bother looking out at her to see whether she was dozing or awake.

"All right," was the last thing he said. "Don't get frightened now. Just keep your head about you, and everything'll pan out. See you in a month." They exchanged a kiss. A blood-red kiss of death.

Then they went out of the kitchen, back into the living-room. They opened the side door of that, came out into the hall. The front door opened and closed again and Janet Miller was left alone in the house—with her knowledge and the potential murderess of her son.

Vernon Miller was a genial, easy-going, goodhearted, unsuspicious sort of man, the kind that so often draws a woman like Vera to be his life partner. He was no easy mark, no sap. He was wary enough in business, in the outside world of men and affairs could even be implacable, hard-boiled, if the occasion warranted. The trouble was, he let his defenses down in the wrong place—laid himself wide open in the home.

Janet Miller heard his key in the door. He said "Hello, there!" to the house in general. Vera came down the stairs, and Janet Miller heard them exchange a kiss. A Judas kiss.

Then he came on out to the back porch, to see her, and

the third component of her trinity, the sound of his voice, was vouchsafed her.

"Did you enjoy the sun?"

Her eyes.

"Want me to take you in now?"

Her terrible eyes.

"Look what I brought you."

Her eyes, her terrible imploring eyes.

"Did you miss me? Glad I'm back? Is that why you're looking at me like that?" He squatted down to the level of the chair, cupped his hand to his knees. "What're you trying to tell me, darling?"

Her eyes, her haunted eyes.

"Shall I try for you? Blink them once for no, twice for yes." This was an old established code between them, their only link. "Are you hungry?" No. "Are you chilly?" No. "Are you—"

Vera called out from the kitchen, interrupted them as if guessing what Janet was trying to do: "Don't stay out there all night, Vern. I'm all ready for you."

Her eyes, her despairing eyes.

He straightened up, shifted around behind the chair, out of her sight, and rolled her into the living-room ahead of him. Left her there for a minute while he went upstairs.

Even her only weapon, the use of her eyes, was blunted, for they almost always followed him around a room, in and out of doors, even on other nights when they had no terrible message to deliver, so how could he be expected to tell the difference tonight?

Vera finished setting the table. "All right, Vern," she called up.

He came down again, hands freshly washed, guided her chair into the dining room, pushed it close up beside Vera at the table, sat down opposite them. Vera was the one who always fed her.

He opened his napkin, looked down, began to spoon soup.

Vera broke the brief preliminary silence. "She won't open her mouth."

She was trying to force a spoonful through Janet Miller's clenched teeth. Janet Miller had retained just enough muscular control of her jaws still to be able to close or slightly relax her mouth, sufficiently to take food. It was tightly shut now.

He looked over at her and she blinked at him. Singly, three times. No, no, no.

"Don't you feel well? Don't you want any?"

"She's just being stubborn," Vera said. "She was perfectly all right all day."

Yes, I was, thought Janet Miller harrowingly, until you let death into my son's house.

She kept trying to force the spoon through. Janet Miller resisted it. It tilted and the soup splashed off. "Now look at that!" she exclaimed short-temperedly.

"Do you want me to feed you?" he asked.

She couldn't signal those three double blinks fast enough. Yes, yes, yes.

He got up and moved the wheelchair around beside his own.

Vera began to apply herself to her own meal with a muttered: "You can have the job; see if I care."

So far so good. She was over beside him now, in closer contact. So near and yet so far. Her pitiful, desperate plan was first to rivet his attention to the fact that something was wrong, something was troubling her, and hold it there. That was the easiest part of it. Once that was accomplished, she must find some way of centering his interest on that oven wherein the two gas masks lay concealed. Get him to go to it, open it himself if possible. Failing that, get him to force Vera to go to it, open it.

In such event Vera would undoubtedly attempt to smuggle them out of their hiding place, find another for them without letting him see her do it. But they were large, bulky, not easily concealed. The chances of his discovering them would be that much greater. Even if he did discover them, that by no means guaranteed that he would understand their implication, realize they meant his own intended death. Vera would probably find some explanation to fob off on him. But she might lose her nerve, it might result in a postponement if nothing else. Lacking speech with which to warn him, that was the most Janet Miller could hope for.

So she took the long, devious, roundabout path that was the only one open to her, to try to focus his attention on the gas oven—by refusing to touch, one by one, all the dishes that had been prepared on the open burners on top of the stove.

"She's not touching a thing," he said finally. He put his hand solicitously to her forehead, to feel if she had a temperature. It was moist with anguish.

"Don't humor her so much," Vera snapped. "There's nothing the matter with this food."

"What is it, dear, aren't you hungry?" She'd been waiting for that! She gave him the yes-signal an infinite number of times.

"She is hungry!" he said in surprise.

"Then why doesn't she eat what's put before her?" Vera said furiously.

"Maybe she wants something special."

Step two! Oh, if it only kept up like this. If she was only given the chance to save him . . .

"I like that," sniffed Vera disdainfully. She was still not on guard against her. As soon as that happened, Janet Miller knew, it would double her difficulties.

He leaned toward her tenderly. "Do you want something special, dear? Something that's not on the table?"

Yes, yes, yes, yes, came her agonized messages.

"See, I knew it!" he said triumphantly.

"Well, she's not going to get it," Vera snapped.

He gave her a rebuking look. All he said, mildly but firmly, was: "Yes, she is." But his meaning was plain—

"would you deprive anyone so unfortunate of a little thing like that, if you knew it would make her a little happier?"

Vera saw she'd gone too far. She tried to cover up her blunder. "How you going to tell what it is, anyway?" she asked sulkily.

"I'll make it my business to," he said, a little coldly.

Janet Miller's thoughts were racing ahead. Many things could be prepared in that oven, but most of them, roasts, pies, and so forth were out of the question, needed long cooking ahead. It must be something that could only be made in there, and yet would not take any time. It held a wire rack in it, a grill. That was it! Bacon. That could be made almost instantly, and there was always some in the house.

He was patiently running through a list of delicacies, trying to arrive at the right one by a process of elimination. "Do you want croquettes?" No. "Succotash?" No—

"Meantime your own meal is getting cold," Vera observed sarcastically. Her nerves were a little on edge, with what she knew lay ahead. She was not ordinarily so heartless about Janet, to give her her due. Or rather she was, but took good pains to keep it concealed from him. His mother could have told him a different story of what went on in the daytime, when he wasn't home.

He began to run out of food names; his suggestions came slower, were about ready to falter to a stop. Fear stabbed at her. She widened her eyes at him imploringly to go on.

Vera came to her aid without meaning to. "It's no use, Vern," she said disgustedly. "Are you going to keep this up all night?"

Her latent opposition only served to solidify his determination, spurred him on to further attempts. "I'm not going to let her go away from this table hungry!" he said stubbornly, and started in again, this time with breakfast dishes, for he had run out of supper ones. "Cereal?" No. "Ham and eggs?" No. Oh, how close he was getting. "Bacon?"

Yes, yes, yes, went her eyes. Her heart sang a paean of

gratitude.

He smacked his palm down on the table in vindication.

"I knew I'd get it finally."

Her eyes left him, shifted appraisingly over to Vera. All the color had drained from her face; it was white as the tablecloth before her. The two women, the mother and the wife, the would-be savior and the would-be killer, exchanged a long measured look. "So you heard us!" was in Vera's look. "So you know." And then with cruel, easily read derision, "Well, try to tell him. Try to save him."

He said plaintively: "You heard what she wants, Vera. What're you sitting there for? Go out and broil her a few strips."

Vera's face was that of a trapped thing. She swallowed, though she hadn't been chewing just then. "I should say not. I got one meal ready. I'm not going to get up in the middle of it and start another! It'll get the stove all greasy and—and—"

He threw his napkin down. "I'll do it myself then. That's one of the few things I do know how to cook—bacon." But before he could move she had shot up from her chair, streaked over toward the doorless opening that led to the kitchen, as though something were burning in there.

"Can't you take a joke?" she said thickly. "What kind of a wife d'you take me for? I wouldn't let you, after you've been working hard all day. Won't take a minute . . ."

He was so defenseless, so unguarded—because he thought he'd left all antagonists outside the front door. He fell for it, grinned amiably after her.

Oh, if he'd only keep looking, only keep watching her from where he was! He could see the oven door from where he was sitting. He could see what she'd have to take out of it in another minute, right from in here. But there was no suspicion in his heart, no thought of treachery. He turned back toward Janet again, smiled into her face reassuringly, patted one of her nerveless hands.

For once her eyes had no time for him. They kept staring

past him into the lighted kitchen. If only he'd turn and follow their direction with his own!

She saw Vera glance craftily out at them first, measuring
her chances of remaining undetected in what she was about
to do. Then she crouched down, let out the oven flap. Then
she looked again, to make sure the position of his head
hadn't shifted in the meantime. Then she crushed the two
bulky olive-drab masks to her, turned furtively away with
them so that her back was to the dining room, sidled across
the room that way, sidewise, and thrust them up into a seldom-used cupboard where preserves were kept.

So it hadn't been just an evil dream. There was murder in
the house with them. Janet Miller's eyes hadn't been idle
while the brief transfer was occurring. They had shifted
frantically from Vera to him, from him to Vera, trying to
draw his own after them, to look in there.

She failed. He misunderstood, thought she was simply
impatient for the bacon. "You'll have it in a minute now,"
he soothed, but he kept on eating his own meal without
looking into the kitchen.

Vera came in with it finally, and the smile she gave Janet
Miller was not a sweet, solicitous one as he thought, it was a
she-devil's smile of mockery and refined cruelty. She knew
Janet had seen what she'd done in there just now, and she
was taunting her with her inability to communicate it to him.

"Here we are," she purred. "Nice and crispy, done to a
turn!"

"Thanks, Vera." The doomed man smiled up at her
gratefully.

The meal finished, he retired to the living-room to read
his paper, wheeled her with him. Vera, with a grim, gloating
look at her, went back into the kitchen to wash the dishes.

Janet Miller's eyes were on his face the whole time they
sat in there alone, but he wouldn't look up at her; he remained buried in the market reports and football results.
Oh, to have a voice—even the hoarsest whispered croak—

what an opportunity, the two of them in there alone like that! But then if she'd had one, the opportunity wouldn't have been given to her. She probably wouldn't have been allowed to overhear in the first place.

Even so, Vera was taking no chances on any circuitous system of communication by trial and error, such as he had used at the table to find out what she wanted. Twice she came as far as the living-room door, stood there and looked in at them for a moment, dishcloth in her hand, on some excuse or other.

His doomed head remained lowered to his paper, oblivious of the frenzied eyes that bored into him, beat at him like electric pulses to claim his attention.

Vera directed an evil smile at the helpless woman at his side, returned whence she had come, well content.

Time was so precious, and it was going so fast. Once Vera came in here with them finally, she'd never leave them again for the rest of the evening.

He felt her imploring eyes on him once, reached out and absently stroked her veined hand without looking up, but that was the closest she got to piercing his unawareness. A football score, a bond quotation, a comic strip, these things were dooming him to death.

Vera came in to them at last, helped herself to a cigarette from his coat pocket, turned on the radio. He looked up at her, said: "Oh, by the way, did you phone the gas company to send a man around to look at that hot-water heater in the bathroom? I'd like to take a bath tonight."

A knife of dread went through Janet Miller's heart. So that was how it was going to be done! That defective water heater in the upstairs bathroom. She closed her eyes in consternation, opened them again. She hadn't known until now what to expect—only that it would be gas in some form or other.

Vera snapped her fingers in pretended dismay. "I meant to, and it slipped my mind completely!" she said contritely.

It hadn't. Janet Miller knew. She'd purposely refrained

from reporting it. That was part of their plan, to make it look more natural afterwards. An unavoidable accident.

"We've used it this long, once more can't hurt," she said reassuringly.

"I know, but it's dangerous the way that thing leaks when you turn it on. We're all liable to be overcome one of these nights. If a man wants anything done around here he's got to attend to it himself," he grumbled.

"I'll notify them the first thing in the morning," she promised submissively.

But there wouldn't be any morning for him.

A moment later she artfully took his mind off the subject by calling his attention to something on the radio. "Did you hear that just then? That was a good one! Don't let's miss this—I think those two are awfully funny."

A joke on the radio. What could be more harmless than that? Yet it was helping to kill a man.

A station announcement came through—"Ten p.m., Eastern Standard Time—"

"Things are picking up. If they keep on like this, I think we'll be able to take that cruise next summer."

No you won't, Janet Miller screamed at him in terrible silence; you're going to be killed tonight! Oh, why can't I make you hear me?

The station announcement came through again. It seemed to her like only a minute since they'd heard the last one. "Ten thirty p.m., Eastern Standard Time—"

He yawned comfortably. "Before you know it the holidays'll be here. What do you want for Christmas?"

"Anything you want to give me," she simpered demurely.

He turned and looked at Janet, then scrutinized her more closely. "What's the matter, dear? Why, there are beads of sweat on your forehead." He came over, took his handkerchief and gently touched them off one by one.

But Vera quickly jumped into the breach. She was on her guard now. Janet had her to combat as well as her own incapacity. The odds were insuperable. "The room is too close, that's all it is. I feel it myself . . ." Vera pretended to mop her own brow.

He reached down and touched Janet's hands.

"But her hands are so cold! That can't be it—"

"Oh, well—" Vera dropped her eyes tactfully. "Her circulation, you know," she murmured under her breath, as if trying not to hurt the paralytic's feelings.

He nodded, satisfied.

Janet's eyes clung to him desperately. Hear me! Why can't you hear me! Why can't you understand what I'm trying so hard to tell you!

He got up, stretched. "I think I'll go up and light that thing, get ready for my bath and go to bed. I had a tough day."

"I think we may as well all go up," Vera said accommodatingly. "There's nothing but swing on all the stations from now on and it gets monotonous." The dial-light snapped out. On such a casual, everyday, domestic note began the preparations for murder.

He picked Janet carefully up in his arms and started for the stairs with her. Her chair was always left downstairs. It was too bulky to be taken up at nights.

She thought distractedly, while the uncarpeted oak steps ticked off beneath him one by one, "Who'll carry me down in the morning? Oh, my son, my son, where will you be then?"

On the stairs their two faces were closer together than at other times. Her frozen lips strained toward him, striving to implant a kiss. He said jocularly: "What are you breathing so hard for? I'm doing all the work."

He carried her into her own room, set her down on the bed, promised, "I'll be in to say good night to you in a minute," and went out to start heating the water for his bath.

It was Vera who always prepared her for bed.

She never needed to be completely undressed, for she no longer wore street clothing, only a warm woolen robe and felt slippers. It was simply a matter of taking these off and arranging the bed coverings about her.

Vera came in and attended to the task as inscrutably, as matter-of-factly, as though there were no knowledge shared between them of what was to happen tonight. This woman bending over her was worse than a murderess. She was a monster, not human at all. Janet's eyes were beseeching her, trying to say to her: "Don't do this; don't take him from me." It was useless; it was like appealing to granite. There were two impulses there too strong to be deflected, overcome—passion for another man, and greed. Pity didn't have a chance.

He was in the bathroom now. There was the soft thud of ignited gas. He called in, just as Vera finished arranging Janet in bed: "Hey, Vera! Do you think it's all right to light this thing? There must be a whale of a leak in it. The flame is more white than blue, with the air in it!" There was a faint but distinct hum coming from the hot-water heater. That, however, was not a sign of its being defective, but a normal accompaniment to its being used.

"Of course it's all right," Vera called back unhesitatingly. "Don't be such a sissy! You'd better not put off taking that bath tonight. You're always too rushed in the morning, and then raise hob with me!"

A thread of acrid warning drifted into Janet's bedroom, dissolved unnoticeably after a single stab at her nostrils. Vera had gone into their bedroom to begin undressing herself. He came in to Janet, in bathrobe and slippers, and he looked so young, so vigorous—to die this soon! He said: "I'll say good night to you now, hon. You must be tired and want to go to sleep."

Then as he bent toward her to kiss her forehead, he saw something, stopped short. He changed his mind, sat down on the edge of the bed instead, kept looking at her steadily. "Vera," he called over his shoulder, "come in here a minute."

She came, the murderess, in pink satin and foamy lace,

like an angel of destruction, stroking her loosened hair with a silver-backed brush.

"What is it now?" She said it a little jumpily.

"Something's troubling her, Vera. We've got to find out what it is. Look, there are tears in her eyes. Look, see that big one, rolling down her cheek?"

Vera's face was a little tense with fear. She forced it into an expression of sympathetic concern, but she had an explanation ready to throw at him, to forestall further inquiry. "Well after all, Vern," she said in an undertone, close to his ear, as though not wanting Janet to overhear her, "it's only natural she should feel that way every once in a while. She has every reason to. Don't forget, we've gotten used to—what happened to her, but it must come back to her every so often." She gave his shoulder a soothing little pat. "That's all it is," she whispered.

He was partly convinced, but not entirely. "But she doesn't take it so hard other nights. Why should she tonight? Ever since I came home tonight she's been watching me so. I've had the strangest feeling at times that she's trying to tell me something . . ."

There was no mistaking the pallor on Vera's face now, but it could so easily have been ascribed to concern about the invalid's welfare, to a wifely sharing of her husband's anxiety.

"I think I'll sit with her awhile," he said.

Yes, stay in here with me, pleaded the woman on the bed, stay in here, stay awake, and nothing can happen to you.

Vera put her arms considerately about his shoulders, gently raised him to his feet. "No, you go in and take your bath. The water must be hot now. I'll sit with her. She'll be all right in the morning, you'll see."

But he won't, my son won't.

Vera threw her a grimace meant to express kindly understanding, as he turned and padded out of the room. "She's just a little downhearted, that's all."

She moved over to the window, stood looking out with

her back to the room. She couldn't bear to face those accusing eyes on the bed. There was a muffled sound of splashing coming through the bathroom door, and then after a while he came out.

"Sure you turned that thing off now?" Vera called in to him warningly. A warning not meant to save, and that couldn't save.

"Yeah," he said through the folds of a towel, "but you can notice the gas odor distinctly. We've got to get that thing fixed the first thing tomorrow. I'm not going to shut myself up in there with it any more. How's Mom?"

"*Shh!* I've got her to sleep already. No, don't go in, you'll only wake her." She reached up, treacherously snapped the light out.

No! Let me say good-bye to him at least! If I can't save him, at least let me see him once more before you—

The door ebbed silently, remorselessly closed, cutting her off. Help! Help! ran the demented whirlpool of her thoughts.

There was the murmured sound of their two voices coming thinly through the partition wall for a while. Then a window sash going up. Then the muted snap of the light switch on their side. It seemed she could hear everything through the paper-thin wall. Not even that was to be spared her. Sweat poured down her face, though a cool fresh night wind was blowing in through her own open window.

Silence. Silence that crouched waiting, like an animal ready to pounce. Silence, that pounded, throbbed like a drum. Silence that went on and on, and almost gave birth to hope, it was so protracted.

Then a very slight sound from in there, barely distinguishable at all—the slither of a window sash coming down to the bottom, sealing the room up.

Her own door opened softly, and a ghostly white-gowned form slithered silently past along the wall, lowered the window in here, stuffed rags around its frame. She must have had the water heater turned on for quite some time already—without being lit this time, of course. The sharp, pungent, acrid odor of illuminating gas drifted in after her, thickened momentarily. She slipped out again, on her errand of death.

One of the lower steps of the staircase, far below, creaked slightly at her passage. Even the slight grinding of the oven door, as it came open, reached Janet Miller's straining ears in the stillness. She must have put them back in there again, while she was washing the dishes.

The odor thickened. Janet Miller began to hear a humming in her ears, at first far away, then drawing nearer, nearer, like a train rushing onward through a long echoing tunnel. He coughed, moaned a little in his sleep, on the other side of the wall. Sleep that was turning into death. He must be getting the effects worse in there. He was nearer the bath, nearer the source of annihilation.

The form glided into Janet's room again. It looked faintly bluish now, not white any more, from the gas refraction. Janet Miller wanted to be sick at her stomach. There was a roaring in her ears. A train was rushing through her skull, in one side out the other now—and the room was lurching around her.

She was pulled up from the pillow she rested on, a voice seemed to say from miles away, "I guess you've had enough to fool them," and something came down over her head. Suddenly she could breathe pure sweet air again. The roaring held steady for a while, then began receding, as if the train were going in reverse now. It died away at last. The blue dimness went out too.

My son! My son!

Through two round goggles she saw the light of dawn come filtering strangely into the room about her. A wavering figure appeared before them presently, one arm out to support herself against the wall as she advanced. Vera, wavering not because Janet Miller's vision was defective any longer, but because the quantity of gas accumulated in the airtight rooms was beginning to affect her, even in the short time since she'd taken off her own mask. She held a wet handkerchief pressed to her mouth in its place, and was evidently striving to hold her breath.

She had sense enough to go over to the window first, remove the rags, open it a little from the bottom before she came back to the bed, reared Janet up to a sitting position and fumblingly pulled the mask off her.

The humming started up again in Janet's ears, the train was coming back toward her.

Vera was gagging into the handkerchief. "Hold your breath all you can, until I get back here," she sobbed. "I'm telling you this for your own sake." She trailed the mask after her by its nozzle, went tottering in a zigzag course out of the room.

Janet Miller could hear her floundering, rather than walking, down the stairs. A door far at the back of the house opened, stayed that way.

The humming kept on increasing for a little while, but then drifts of uncontaminated air from the open window began knifing their way in, neutralized it. Gas must still be pouring out of the heater in the bath down the hall, however.

Hold your breath as much as you can, she had said just now. That was to live, though. He's gone, Janet Miller thought. He must be by now, or she wouldn't have come in here to take the mask off me. Maybe I can go with him, that's the best thing for me to do now. She began to take great deep breaths, greedily draw in all the poisoned air she could, hold it in her lungs. Like going under it purposely, in a dentist chair, when they gave you a breath count.

The humming advanced on her again, became a deep-throated roar. The room became a dark-blue pinwheel, spinning madly, rapidly darkening around its edges as it spun.

"We'll fool them, Vern, we'll go together," she thought hazily. The darkness had reached the center of the pinwheel now; only a pinpoint of blue remained at its exact core. Glass tinkled somewhere far off, but that had nothing to do with her.

The pinpoint of blue went out and there was nothing.

She was very thirsty and she kept drinking air. Such delicious air. It poured down her and she couldn't get enough of it. She couldn't see anything. She was inside a big tent, something like that anyway, but she could hear a murmur of voices. Then there was a blinding flash of light and the delicious flow of air stopped for a minute. Then the kindly darkness returned, the flow of air resumed.

"She's coming up. She'll be all right."

"Wonderful, isn't it? You'd think just a whiff of it, anyone in her condition—"

The flash of light repeated itself. Then again, and again, faster and faster all the time, like a flickering movie film, and suddenly it stayed on permanently, there was no more darkness, and her eyes were open.

She was violently sick and, although she thought that was a bad thing, the faces all around her looked on encouragingly and nodded, as though it were a very good thing.

"She's O.K. now. Nothing more to worry about."

"How're the other two?" someone called inside to another room.

"The wife's O.K.," the voice of somebody unseen answered. "The husband's gone."

They picked her up—she must have been on a stretcher—and started to carry her out. Just before they left the room with her, a desolate screaming started up somewhere within the house. "No, no, don't stop! Bring him back! You must! Oh, why couldn't it have been me instead? Why did it have to be him?"

They carried Janet Miller out and put her into the back of an automobile, and she didn't hear any more of the screaming.

*   *   *

A pallid, mournful figure came into the room with the nurse. It was hard to recognize Vera in the widow's weeds. This was two days later.

"You're going home now, dear," the nurse told Janet Miller cheerfully. "Here's your daughter-in-law come to take you back with her."

Janet Miller blinked her eyes. No, no, no. It was no use. They didn't know the old code she and Vern had had.

"Can you manage it?" the nurse asked Vera.

"I have a friend waiting downstairs with a car. If you'll just have somebody wheel the chair down for me, we can take her right in it with us."

She was taken down in an elevator, still blinking futilely, rolled out to the hospital driveway by the orderly, and a man got out of a sedan waiting there. So now she saw her son's other murderer for the first time.

He was taller than Vern had been and better-looking, much better-looking, but his face was weaker, didn't have as much character in it—the kind that the Veras of this world go to hell for.

He and the orderly lifted her out of the chair and got her onto the front seat of the car. Then the chair was fastened to the outside, in back. It was too bulky to go inside the car.

Vera got in next to her—she was between the two of them now—and they drove away from the hospital. She hadn't been kept there all this time because of the gas, of course, but simply so she could be cared for properly during the first, acute stages of Vera's "grief."

"That cost plenty!" Vera said explosively as the hospital receded behind them.

"It looked good though, didn't it?" he argued. "Anyway, what the hell. We've got plenty of it now, haven't we?"

"All right, but why waste it on her? What're we going to do, have her hanging around our necks like a millstone from now on?"

The shoulders of both of them were pressed against hers, one on each side, yet they spoke back and forth as though she were five miles away, without pity for her helplessness.

"She's our immunity. How many times do I have to tell you that? So long as she stays with us, under the same roof, looked after by us, there won't be a whisper raised. We gotta have her around—for a while anyway."

Vera flipped back her widow's veil, put a cigarette in her mouth. "I'll have time for just one before we get up to our own neighborhood. Gee, I'll be glad when this sob-act is over!"

She threw the cigarette out of the car, lowered the veil again, as they turned down the street that led to the house that had belonged to Janet Miller's son. A residue of smoke came through the mesh of the veil, made her look like the monster she was.

Vera went in first, head bowed in case the neighbors were looking. He carried Janet in his arms, came back for the chair and took that in afterwards.

"Now come on, clear out," Vera said to him as soon as Janet had been installed in it. "You can't begin to hang around here yet; they may be watching."

"Let me get a pick-up, at least," he growled aggrievedly. "What's the idea of the bum's rush?" He downed two fingers of Vern's brandy with a single streamlined motion, from decanter to tumbler to mouth.

"I thought you were the one wanted to be careful. We gotta take it easy."

She came back into the room again after she'd sped him on his way, slung off her widow's hat and veil. She found Janet's eyes fastened on her remorselessly, like two bright stones.

She helped herself to a drink like he had, a little jerkily, not quite so streamlined. "Now I'm going to tell you one thing," she flared out at her unexpectedly. "If you want to stay out of trouble, keep those eyes of yours off me. Quit staring at me all the time! I know what you're thinking. You may as well forget it; it won't do you any good!"

*   *   *

His visits increased in number and lengthened in duration each time until, about three weeks after they'd brought her back from the hospital, they were married. They didn't announce it, of course, but Janet Miller heard them talking about it when they came home one day, and he didn't leave the house again from then on. He just moved in with them, so she knew what it meant. She found out what his name was then, too, for the first time. Haggard, Jimmy Haggard. Murderer of Vernon Miller.

The community at large would probably think it was one of those "whirlwind" courtships. Young widow alone in world turns to only person who has shown her sympathy in her distress—very natural. Its haste might shock them, but then after all, another three or four weeks would elapse before it could be definitely confirmed, and by then it would seem that much less abrupt.

Janet Miller lived in a state of suspended animation for a while, a trancelike condition between being dead and alive. She undoubtedly drew breath and imbibed nourishment, so technically she was alive, but little more than that could be said for her. Not only the voice was gone now, but the other two primaries had gone with it—the sun and the blue sky. None of the three would ever return again. And so she would surely have died within a month or two at the most, for sheer lack of will to live, when slowly but surely a spark ignited, a new vital force began to glow sullenly, taking the place of the three that had vanished. Revenge.

From a spark it became a flame, from a flame an all-consuming conflagration. She was more alive now than she had ever been since her disabling catastrophe had overtaken her. Fiercely it burned, by day, by night. It needed no replenishment, no renewal. Time meant nothing to it. Hours meant nothing, days meant nothing, years meant nothing. She would wait. She would live to be a hundred, if need be, but she would wreak her retribution on this pair before she went. Surely, inescapably. Someday, somehow.

They played into her hands. They found her a burden, a

nuisance. They began to bicker and quarrel about her. Neither one wanted to be annoyed moving her chair or feeding her. He had more humanity than the woman. No, that was not it either—not real humanity, consideration. It was just that he was less reckless than Vera, more craven.

"But we can't just let her starve, and she can't feed herself! She'll die on our hands for lack of attention, and then they're liable to find out we neglected her, and one thing'll lead to another, and first thing you know they'll reopen the other thing, start putting two and two together, asking questions."

"Well then, hire somebody to look after her. I'm not staying home all the time to spoon mush into her mouth, tuck her into bed! Get a companion for her. We've got dough enough for that now. Or else get rid of her altogether, farm her out to some nursing home."

"No, not yet. We gotta keep her with us a few months, at least, until we've cooled off," he insisted. "And yet I don't like the idea of letting a stranger in here with us. It's kind of risky. Especially somebody from the neighborhood that used to know Miller. We've got to be careful. One of us is liable to shoot our mouths off when we've got a lot of booze in us."

While he was trying to make up his mind whether or not to take a chance, advertise or go to an agency, the matter was decided for him by one of those fortuitous coincidences that sometimes happen. A well-spoken young fellow, apparently down on his luck, was passing by one morning, and seeing Haggard on the front porch, approached timorously and asked if there was any work he could do, such as mowing the lawn or washing the windows. He explained that he was hitchhiking his way across country, and had just reached town half an hour before. As a matter of fact, he was packing a small bundle with him, apparently the sum total of his worldly goods.

Haggard looked him over speculatively. Then he glanced at the old lady. That seemed to give him an idea. "Come in a minute," he said.

Janet Miller could hear him talking to him in the living-room. Then he called Vera down and consulted with her. She seemed to approve—probably only too glad to have someone take the old lady off their hands.

She brought him outside with her right after that, minus his bundle now.

"Here she is," she said curtly. "Now you understand what's required, don't you? We'll be out a good deal. You've got to spoon-feed her, and don't take any nonsense from her. She's got a cute little habit of going on hunger strikes. Pinch her nose until she has to open her mouth for air, if you have any trouble with her. You sleep out, but get here about nine so you can take her down on the porch. You don't need to worry about dressing her, just wrap her in a blanket if I'm not up. Take her back to her room at night, after she's been fed. That's about all there is to it. I want someone in the house with her while we're out, just to see that nothing happens."

"Yes ma'am," he said submissively.

"All right—what's your name again?"

"Casement."

"All right, Casement. Mr. Haggard's already told you what you're to get. That about covers everything. You can consider yourself hired. Bring out a chair for yourself, if you want one."

He sat down to one side of the rubber-tired wheelchair, where he could watch her, hands on knees, legs apart.

They looked at each other, the old woman and the young man.

He smiled a little at her, tentatively. She could read sympathy behind it. She sensed, somehow, that this was his first case of the kind, that he'd never come into contact with anything like this before.

After about half an hour he got up, said, "I think I'll get a glass of water. You want one too?" as though she could have answered. Then remembering that she couldn't, he stood there at a loss, looking at her. He was very inexperienced at a job like this; that could be seen with half an eye. He mumbled, half to himself, "How'm I going to tell when you . . ." Then rubbed his neck baffledly.

He turned and went inside anyway. He came out again in a minute, bringing one for her. He carried it over to her and stood with it, looking down at her uncertainly. She blinked her eyes twice to show him she was thirsty. To show him— if possible—a little more than that. He held it to her lips and slowly let its contents trickle into her mouth until it was empty.

"Want any more?" he asked.

She blinked once this time.

He put the glass down on the floor and stood looking at her, thoughtfully stroking his chin. "Sometimes you blink twice in a hurry, sometimes you just blink once. What is that for, yes and no? Well now, let's find out just to make sure." He picked up a newspaper, found the word "yes" in it, held his finger under it and showed it to her. She blinked twice. Then he found a "no," showed that to her. She blinked once.

"Well, now we're that much ahead, aren't we?" he said cheerfully.

Her eyes seemed to be smiling—they were very expressive eyes. The code—she had her old code with Vern back again, as easy as that! He was a very smart young man.

The afternoon waned. He pushed her chair in to the supper table, sat and spooned her food to her mouth for her, a little awkwardly at first, but he soon got the hang of it, learned he must not load the spoon too much, as her jaws could only open to a limited extent.

Vera gave him a look. "You seem to have better luck with her than we did ourselves. She'll swallow for you, at least."

"Sure," he said comfortably without taking his eyes from what he was doing, "Mrs. Miller and I are going to be great friends."

Janet Miller couldn't account for it, but he had spoken the truth. She could feel a sense of confidence, almost of alliance with him, without knowing why.

He carried her up to her room later and she didn't see him any more that night. But she lay there in the dark, content. The flame burned high, unquenchable. Perhaps . . .

In the morning he came up to get her, carried her downstairs, gave her orange juice to drink, and sat with her on the front porch. For a while he just sat, basking as she was. Then presently he turned his head and glanced behind him at the front windows of the house, as if to ascertain whether anyone was in those rooms or not. But the way he did it was so casual she didn't read any meaning into it. Perhaps he was just thinking to himself that the Haggards were late risers.

He said in a rather low voice, almost an undertone: "Do you like Mr. Haggard?"

Her eyes snapped just once, like a blue electric spark.

He waited awhile, then he said: "Do you like Mrs. Haggard?"

The negative blink this time was almost ferocious.

"I wonder why," he said slowly, but it didn't sound like a question.

That sense of alliance, of confederacy, came over her again, stronger than ever. Her eyes were fastened on him hopefully.

"It's too bad we can't talk," he sighed and relapsed into silence.

Vera came downstairs, and then presently Haggard followed her. They began to bicker and their voices were clearly audible out on the porch.

"I gave you fifty only last night!" she snarled. "Go easy, will you?"

"What're you trying to do, keep me on an allowance?"

"Whose money is it, anyway?"

"If it wasn't for me, you—"

There was a warning "*Sh!*" followed by, "Don't forget the old lady ain't by herself out there no more."

The sudden restraint spoke more eloquently than any reckless revelation could have. Janet Miller's eyes were on Casement's face. He gave not the slightest sign of having heard anything that surprised him.

Haggard went out to get the car, brought it around to the front door. Vera came out, threw Casement a careless "You know what to do," and got in. They drove off.

Almost before they were out of sight down the long tree-lined street, he'd got up and gone inside. Not hurriedly or furtively, simply as though he had something to do that couldn't be postponed any longer.

He stayed in there a long time. She could hear him first in one room, then in another. He seemed to go through the entire house upstairs and down while he was about it. She could hear a drawer slide open from time to time, or a desk-flap being let down. If it hadn't been for that peculiar, inexplicable confidence with which he seemed to inspire her, she might have thought him a burglar who had taken the job just for an opportunity to ransack the house in its owners' absence. Somehow the idea never occurred to her.

He came back outside again finally, after almost an hour, shaking his head slightly to himself. He sat down beside her, reached into his inside pocket, took out a little oblong book—a pocket dictionary.

"You and I have got to find some way of getting beyond yes and no," he murmured. "I'd like to talk to you. That's why I wangled this job."

He glanced out between the porch posts, across the front lawn, up and down the sunny street. There was no one in sight. He took something from his vest pocket. Janet Miller thought it was a watch for a minute, until she saw that it was shield-shaped, not round. It had the State seal engraved on it. He let her see it, then put it away again. "I'm a detective,"

he said. "I came up here and examined the premises immediately after it happened, just in the line of duty. Mrs. Haggard, as I at first reconstructed it, was awakened by the gas,
managed to stagger down to the floor below, break the glass
pane in the front door, then get over to the phone to try and
call for help. She only had strength left to take the receiver
off, then fell down with it and was found there on the floor
by the telephone, overcome.

"However, I happened to question the switchboard operator who had sent in the alarm, and she insisted it was the
other way around. She distinctly heard the crash of glass,
over the open wire, *after* the receiver was already off. That
made it a little hard to understand. That was a plate-glass
inset in that door, not just thin window glass. She had to
swing a heavy andiron at it to shatter it. Now if a person is
not even strong enough to whisper 'Help' over the phone,
how in the world is she able to crash out a solid square of
plate glass?

"Furthermore, once she was at the door why did she turn
around and go all the way back to the phone, which was
already disconnected, and fall down there? There is a considerable length of hall between the two. It wasn't at the
door she was found, you understand, it was at the *phone*.

"As peculiar as that struck me, I think I would have let it
go by, but I visited the hospital while she was there being
treated and asked to see her things. The light satin bedroom
slippers she'd had on were discolored around the edges
from dew, and I found traces of moist earth and a blade of
grass adhering to their soles. She'd been *outside the house* before she was overcome, then went in again, closed the door
after her, and smashed the glass panel in it from the inside.

"Then on top of all that, the usual neighborhood gossip
has begun to drift in to us, about how soon afterwards she
and Haggard were married. Even an anonymous letter or
two. I tell you all this because, although this is going to be
one of the toughest things I've ever come up against, I think
you may be able to help me before we're through."

*   *   *

She could hardly breathe. The flame leaped heavenward and she blinked her eyes—twice—as rapidly as she could.

"Then there is something you can tell me about it? Good. Well, the main thing I want to know is: did he lose his life accidentally or not?"

No!

He gave her a long look. But she could see there was really no surprise in it, only confirmation. He thumbed the pocket dictionary, put his thumbnail below a word, held it up to her.

"Murder," it read.

Yes.

"By his wife?" His mouth was tightening up a little.

She stopped and thought a minute. If she once set him off on a false scent, or on an only partially correct scent, which was just as bad, there might be no possible way for her to correct him later.

She blinked once. Then immediately afterwards she blinked twice.

"Yes and no?" he said. "What do you mean by . . . ?" Then he got it! He was turning out to be a smart young man, this ally of hers, this Casement. "His wife and some-body else?"

Yes.

"Haggard and your son's wife then, of course."

Yes.

"But—" he said uncertainly. "She was overcome herself."

No.

"She wasn't overcome?"

No.

"But I've seen the report of the ambulance doctor who treated her. I've spoken to him. She was taken to the hospital."

They wasted the rest of the morning over that. She wasn't particularly interested in convincing him that Vera's gas poisoning had been feigned—as a matter of fact, it had only been partially so—but she was vitally interested in keeping him from going past that point, in order to try to bring the gas masks into it. Once he did, she might never again be able to make him understand what method had been used.

They went at it again in the afternoon, on the back porch. "There's something there that seems to be holding us up. How is it you're so sure she wasn't overcome? You were overcome yourself— Sorry, I forgot, I can only ask you questions that shape to a yes or no answer."

He was plainly stumped for a while. Took out some papers from his pocket, reports or jotted notes of some kind, and pored over them for a few minutes.

"He and she were occupying that same room, up there, that the Haggards are using now. You insist she wasn't overcome by the gas. Oh, I see what you mean—she saved herself by doing what I suspected from the looks of those bedroom slippers, stayed outside while the gas was escaping, came back inside again after it had killed your son, avoiding most of its effects in that way. Is that right?"

No.

"She didn't save herself in that way?"

No.

"Did she stay in another room upstairs, with the windows open?"

No.

He was plainly confounded. "She didn't stay in the same room with him, the back bedroom, the whole time the gas was escaping?"

Yes.

He riffled his hair distractedly. She focused her eyes downward on the pocket dictionary he still held in his hand, glared at it as though it were her worst enemy.

Finally he translated the look. "Something in there. Yes, but what word in it?" he asked helplessly.

Why didn't he open it? If he didn't hurry up and open it, he'd lose the thread of the conversation that had immediately preceded her inspiration. She didn't even know whether the word was in there. If it was, she was counting on alphabetical progression. . . .

"Well, we'll get it if it takes all week. She stayed right in the bedroom with him while he was asphyxiated. She wasn't harmed, you insist, and there's some word in here you want. Something about bedrooms?"

No.

"Something about windows?"

No.

"Something about the gas itself?"

Yes! He almost tore the little book in half to get to the G's.

"Gas. We'll take it from there on, all right?"

Instead of blinking, for once, she shut her eyes.

She was saying a prayer.

He started to run his finger down the page, querying her as he went. "Gaseous?" No. "Gastric?" No. "Gastronomy?" No. Suddenly he stopped. He'd seen it himself, automatically; she could tell by the flash of enlightenment that lit up his face.

"Gas mask! Why didn't I think of that myself! It's been as obvious as the nose on my face the whole time!"

Tears of happiness twinkled in her eyes.

"So she saved herself by using a gas mask."

Yes, she told him.

"Did she put one on you, too?"

Yes.

"Very smart angle, there. It would have been too obvious if they'd let you go with him. Who'd she get them from, Haggard?"

Yes, she told him.

"Was he here that night, while it was taking place?"

No.

"Too smart, eh? Well, he's an accessory just the same." He hitched his chair a little closer to her. "Now, you want to see these people punished, of course, Mrs. Miller. He was your son."

How needless was the yes she gave him. The flame of vengeance was a towering pillar of fire now.

"You know they killed your son, and now I know it too. But I've got to have stronger evidence than that. And what other evidence is there but those two gas masks? Everything depends on whether I can recover them or not. You had one on, and she removed it before outsiders arrived, obviously. You must have been conscious at least for a short while after she removed it. Did you see what she did with them?"

Yes.

Technically, she hadn't, of course. But the answer was yes just the same, because she had heard beforehand what they intended doing with them.

"Swell," he breathed fervently, balling a fist. "I suppose we'll have a hard time getting it, but we'll keep at it until we do. Am I tiring you?" he broke off to ask solicitously. "We've got plenty of time, you know. I don't want to hurt you by all this excitement in one day."

Tiring her! The flame of vengeance burned so high, so white, so tireless within her that she could have gone on for hours. No, she signaled.

"All right. About what was done with them afterwards. Let's try a few short cuts. She hid them someplace in the house?"

No.

"I didn't think she would. It would've been too chancy. She hid them someplace outside the house?"

Yes.

"Do you know where?"

Yes.

"But how could you? Excuse me. Let's see. Under one of the porches?"

No.

"The garage?"

She refused to answer yes or no, afraid once more of

sending him off on a wrong trail and being unable to correct it later. He might leave her and go out there and start tearing the garage apart.

"Not the garage then?"

She still refused to answer.

"The garage no answer, and not the garage, no answer either." He got it. Thank heaven for creating smart young men. "The car?"

Yes.

"The one they've got now?"

No.

"They've bought that since. That's down here in my notes. A former car then. Did you hear them discussing it afterwards? Is that how you know?"

No.

"You weren't in a position to see it being done at the time, and you didn't hear them talking it over afterwards. You must have heard them discussing it beforehand then."

Yes.

His face lit up. "That explains the whole thing. How it is you're so hep to what went on. That's swell. Did they know you overheard them?"

She couldn't afford to tell him the truth on that one. It might weaken his credulity. But she was convinced they hadn't deviated in the slightest from the plan she had heard them shape in the kitchen that afternoon, anyhow. No, was her response.

"She doesn't drive." He'd learned that already, probably by watching them come and go. "He came and took the car away for her, then, with the masks still in it? That it?"

She didn't answer.

"I see. He sent someone else up to get it, probably without taking him into their confidence. Therefore the masks must have been concealed in it, and he got them out at the other end without being observed."

Yes.

"He owned a garage and repairshop, didn't he, before his

marriage?" He didn't ask her that; just looked it up in his notes. "Yes, here it is. Ajax Garage and Service Station, Clifford Avenue. I'm going down there and look around thoroughly. There's not much chance that those two masks haven't been destroyed by now. But there is a chance, and a good one, that they were imperfectly destroyed. If I can just turn up sufficient remnants identifiable as having belonged to one or more gas masks, scraps of metal even, that'll do the trick. You've told me all you can, Mrs. Miller, reconstructed the whole thing for me. The rest depends entirely on whether or not I can recover those two masks, intact or in fragments." He put the jotted notes, and the pocket dictionary that had served them so well, back into his coat. "We may get the two of them yet, Mrs. Miller," he promised softly, as he stood up.

The flame of vengeance roared rejoicingly in her own ears. Her eyes were on him meltingly. He seemed to understand what they were trying to say. But then who could have failed to understand, they were so eloquent?

"Don't thank me," he murmured deprecatingly. "It's just part of my job."

Two days went by. He was there to look after her as usual, so he must have been pursuing his investigations at night, after leaving the house, she figured. More than once, when he appeared in the mornings, he looked particularly tired, dozed there on the porch beside her, while her eyes fondly gave his sleeping face their blessing.

There is no hurry, take your time, my right arm, my sword of retribution, she encouraged him silently.

He didn't tell her what success he was having, although the Haggards were out as much as ever and there was plenty of opportunity. It was hard to read his face, to tell whether he was being successful or not. Her eyes clung to him imploringly now, as much as they had ever clung to Vern Miller.

"You want to know, don't you?" he said at last. "You're

eating your heart out waiting to find out, and it'd be cruel to keep you guessing any longer. Well—I haven't had any luck so far. Their car's still there in the garage, held for sale. I practically pulled it apart and put it together again, posing as a prospective buyer. Not while he was around, of course. They're not in it any more. What's more to the point, no one around the garage, no one of the employees, saw him take them out to dispose of them, or saw them at all. I've questioned them all; I haven't any doubts left on that score. I've searched the garage from top to bottom, sifted ashes, refuse, debris, in every vacant lot for blocks around. I've examined the premises where Haggard lived before he moved in here. Not a sign of anything."

He was walking restlessly back and forth between the veranda posts while he spoke.

"Damn the luck anyway!" he spat out. "Those things are bulky. They can't just be made to vanish into thin air. Even if he used corrosive acid, nothing could disappear that thoroughly. He didn't take them out over deep water, send them down to the bottom, because I've checked back on his movements thoroughly. He hasn't been on any ferries or boats, or near any docks or bridges. Where did they come from, where did they go?"

He stopped short, looked at her. "That's it!" he exclaimed. "Why didn't I think of that before? If I can't find out where they went to, maybe I can find out where they came from. I may have better luck if I go at it the other way around. You don't just pick up things like that at the five-and-ten. Did you hear him say where he got them from, when you heard them planning the thing?"

Yes, she answered eagerly.

"Did he buy them?"

No.

"Was he given them?"

No.

"Did he steal them?"

Yes.

"From a factory where they're made?"

No.

"From an Army post?"

No.

He scratched his head. "Where else could he get hold of things like that? From some friend, somebody he knew?"

Yes.

"That doesn't help much. Who is he? Where'd he get them from?"

She stared intently at the morning sun, blinked twice, then her eyes sought his. Then she did it again. Then a third time.

"I don't get you. The sun? He got them from the sun?"

This time she looked slightly lower than the sun, midway between it and the horizon. "The East?" he caught on.

Yes.

"But we're in the East already. Oh—Europe?"

Yes.

"Wait a minute, I know what you mean now. He swiped them from someone who brought them back from there."

Yes.

"That does it!" he cried elatedly. "Now I know how I'll find out who he is! Through the Customs office. He had to declare those things, especially if he brought in several with him at once. They'll be down on his Customs declaration. Now I see too why I haven't been able to find any traces of them in ash heaps or refuse dumps. He must be holding them intact somewhere, waiting his chance to return them if he hasn't already. He'll try to get them back unnoticed to where he got them from. That would be the smartest thing he could do. At last I think we've got a lead, Mrs. Miller—if only it isn't too late!"

The telephone rang out shrilly in the almost total darkness of the room. Casement pushed back his cuff, glanced at the radium dial of his wrist watch. A quarter to twelve. He didn't move, just let it go ahead ringing until it had stopped again of its own accord. He had an idea who it was—trying to find out for sure if there was anyone in this particular house or not. He guessed that if he answered it he wouldn't hear anything—just a click at the other end, and his scheme would have been a failure.

"Not taking any chances, is he?" he grunted to himself. "Even though by now he must have gotten that post card in Hamilton's handwriting I had routed through Boston."

He was longing for a smoke, but he knew better than to indulge in one. The slightest little thing, such as a lighted cigarette glimpsed through the dark windows of this sup- posedly untenanted house could ruin the whole carefully prepared setup. He'd worked too hard and patiently to have that happen now.

He looked at his watch again presently. A quarter after now; half an hour had gone by.

"Due any minute now," he murmured.

Within the next thirty seconds the soft purr of a car run- ning in low sounded from outside. It slowed a little as it came opposite the house, but neither veered in nor stopped. Instead, it went on past toward the next corner, like a ghost under the pale streetlights. He smiled grimly as he recog- nized it. It would go around the block, reconnoitering, then come by a second time and stop. Its occupant was taking every possible precaution but the right one—staying away from here altogether.

The showdown was at hand. Casement finally left the big wing chair he'd sat in ever since dusk, felt for the gun on his hip and moved noiselessly out into the hall. He went back behind the stairs, where there was a door leading into a small storeroom built into the staircase structure itself.

He disappeared in there just as the whirr of wheels ap- proached outside once more, from the same direction as before. This time they stopped. There was a brief wait, then the muffled sound of a car door clicking open. Then a fur- tive footfall from the porch. A key turned in the lock.

Casement nodded to himself at the sound. "Swiped Hamilton's key, evidently. Took a wax impression for a duplicate, and then got it back to him somehow. That's how he got them out of here in the first place."

The door opened and a little gray light from the street filtered into the inky front hall. Through a hairline door-crack at the back of the stairs Casement could make out a looming silhouette standing there, listening. It was empty-handed, but that was all right. He was just taking every precaution.

The silhouette widened the door-opening. Then it bent down, scanning the three-days' accumulation of dummy mail Casement had carefully planted just inside the door, under Hamilton's letter slot. There was also a quart bottle of milk that he'd bought at a dairy standing outside. The inked-in figure straightened, turned around, and descended from the porch again, leaving the door open the way it was. Casement wasn't worried, didn't stir.

There was another wait. Again the porch creaked. The silhouette was back again, this time with a square object like a small-sized suitcase in one hand. The door closed after it and everything became dark again.

Cautious footfalls came along the carpeted hall toward the staircase. They didn't go up it but came on toward the back. He was feeling his way, smart enough not to put on the lights or even use a pocket torch or match in the supposedly untenanted house.

The storeroom door under the stairs that Casement had gone through opened softly. Still nothing happened. There was the sound of something being set down on the floor. Then of two small suitcase latches clicking open one after the other. Then a great rattling of paper being undone, followed by something scratchy being lifted out of the paper.

There were hooks along the wall in there, with various seldom-used things hanging from them. Golf bags, cased tennis rackets—and gas masks that Hamilton had brought back from Europe as souvenirs.

An arm groped upward along the wall, feeling for a vacant hook. Casement had left two conveniently unburdened for just this situation.

The other found it, by sense of touch alone. The arm dipped down again toward the floor, came up with something in it that rustled—and then suddenly there was a sharp metallic click in the stillness of the enclosed little space.

There was a gasp of abysmal terror, something dropped with a thud to the floor, and a light bulb went on overhead, lit up the place wanly.

Haggard and Casement were standing there face to face, across an upended trunk belonging to the house's owner. Haggard was on the outside of it, the detective on the inside, but they were already linked inextricably across the top of it by a manacle whose steel jaws must have been waiting there in the dark the whole time for Haggard to reach toward that empty hook, like bait in a trap.

An olive-drab gas mask lay at Haggard's feet. A second one still nestled in the small suitcase by the storeroom door, waiting to be transferred.

"Pretty," was all Casement said. "It's taken a long time and a lot of work, but it was worth it!" He glanced down at the torn half of a cardboard tag still attached to the handle of the suitcase. "So that's where you had them hidden all the time I was looking for them. Checked in a parcel room somewhere under a phony name, waiting for Hamilton to be away and the coast clear so you could smuggle them back in again unseen. Not a bad idea—if it had only worked."

The sky was blue, the sun was bright, and Janet Miller sat there in her chair on the front porch. She looked at the man and the woman standing before her, each handcuffed to a detective, and the flame within her blazed heavenward, triumphant.

"Take a look at this woman, whose son you murdered," Casement said grimly. "Face those eyes if you can—and deny it."

They couldn't. Haggard's head fell before her gaze. Vera averted hers. They shifted weight uncomfortably.

"You'll see her again. She'll be the principal witness against you—along with Hamilton and his two gas masks. Take them away, boys." He turned her chair around so she could watch them go.

"I guess you wonder how I knew just which night he'd show up there at Hamilton's house," he said to her. "I made sure it'd be last night. I went to Hamilton, told him the whole story, and he agreed to help me. He went to Boston, mailed Haggard a postcard from there day before yesterday. He said he was staying until today. That made last night the only night Haggard would supposedly have had a chance to get those masks back in the house undetected. I faked some mail and filled the letter box with it, and stood a bottle of milk at the door. He fell for it."

An important-looking white-haired man came out of the house, went over to Casement, put his hand on his shoulder. "Great work," he said. "You sure sewed that one up—and singlehanded at that!"

Casement motioned toward Janet Miller. "I was just an auxiliary. Here's where the thanks and the credit go."

"Who'll look after her until the trial comes up?" the captain asked.

"Why, I guess there's room enough over in our house," Casement said.

The sky was blue, the sun was warm, and her eyes shone softly as they rested on him. She had three things to live for again.

THE NIGHT I DIED

The point about me is: that I should stay on the right side of the fence all those years, and then when I did go over, go over heart and soul like I did—all in the space of one night. In one hour, you might say.

Most guys build up to a thing like that gradually. Not me; why, I had never so much as lifted a check, dropped a slug into a telephone-slot before that. I was the kind of a droop who, if I was short-changed, I'd shut up about it, but if I got too much change back I'd stand there and call their attention to it.

And as for raising my hand against a fellow-mortal—you had the wrong party, not Ben Cook. Yet there must have been a wide streak of it in me all along, just waiting to come out. Maybe all the worse for being held down all those years without a valve, like steam in a boiler.

Here I'd been grubbing away for ten or twelve years in Kay City, at thirty per, trying on suits (on other guys) in the men's clothing section of a department store. Saying "sir" to every mug that came in and smoothing their lapels and patting them on the back. I go home one night that kind of a guy, honest, unambitious, wishy-washy, without even a parking-ticket on my conscience, and five minutes later I've got a murder on my hands.

I think it was probably Thelma more than anyone else who brought this latent streak in me to the surface; it might have stayed hidden if she hadn't been the kind of woman she was. You'll see, as you read on, that she had plenty of reason later to regret doing so. Like conjuring up the devil and then not being able to get rid of him.

Thelma was my common-law wife. My first wife, Florence, had given me up as hopeless five years before and gone to England. We parted friends. I remember her saying she liked me well enough, I had possibilities, but it would take too long to work them out; she wanted her husband readymade. She notified me later she'd got a divorce and was marrying some big distillery guy over there.

I could have married Thelma after that, but somehow we never got around to it, just stayed common-law wife and husband, which is as good as anything. You know how opposites attract, and I guess that's how I happened to hook up with Thelma; she was just my opposite in every way. Ambitious, hard as nails, no compunctions about getting what she wanted. Her favorite saying was always, "If you can get away with it, it's worth doing!"

For instance, when I told her I needed a new suit and couldn't afford one, she'd say: "Well, you work in a men's clothing department! Swipe one out of the stock—they'll never know the difference." I used to think she was joking.

After she egged me on to tackle our manager for a raise, and I got turned down pretty, she said: "I can see where you'll still be hauling in thirty-a-week twenty years from now, when they have to wheel you to work in a chair! What about me? Where do I come in if a hit-and-run driver spreads you all over the street tomorrow? Why don't you take out some insurance at least?"

So I did. First I was going to take out just a five-thousand-dollar policy, which was pretty steep for me at that, but Thelma spoke up. "Why not make it worth our while? Don't worry about the premiums, Cookie. I've got a little something put away from before I knew you. I'll start you off. I'll pay the first premium for you myself—after that, we'll see." So I went for ten thousand worth, and made Thelma the beneficiary, of course, as I didn't have any folks or anyone else to look after.

That had been two years before; she had been paying the premiums for me like a lamb ever since. All this made me realize that under her hard surface she was really very big-hearted, and this one night that I started home a little earlier than usual I was warbling like a canary and full of pleasant

thoughts about "my little woman," as I liked to call her, and
wondering what we were going to have for dinner.

Six was my usual quitting-time at the store, but we had
just got through taking inventory the night before, and I had
been staying overtime without pay all week, so the manager
let me off an hour sooner. I thought it would be nice to surprise Thelma, because I knew she didn't expect me for another two or three hours yet, thinking we would still be
taking inventory like other nights. So I didn't phone ahead I
was coming.

Sherrill, who had the necktie counter across the aisle,
tried to wangle me into a glass of suds. If I'd given in, it
would have used up my hour's leeway. I would have got
home at my regular time—and it also would have been my
last glass of suds on this earth. I didn't know that; the reason I refused was I decided to spend my change instead on
a box of candy for her. Sweets to the sweet!

Our bungalow was the last one out on Copeland Drive.
The asphalt stopped a block below. The woods began on
the other side of us, just young trees like toothpicks. I had
to get off at the drug store two blocks down anyway, because the buses turned around and started back there. So I
bought a pound of caramels tied with a blue ribbon, and I
headed up to the house.

I quit whistling when I turned up the walk, so she
wouldn't know I was back yet and I could sneak up behind
her maybe and put my hands over her eyes. I was just full of
sunshine, I was! Then when I already had my key out, I
changed my mind and tiptoed around the house to the back.
She'd probably be in the kitchen anyway at this hour, so I'd
walk in there and surprise her.

She was. I heard her talking in a low voice as I pulled the
screen door noiselessly back. The wooden door behind that
was open, and there was a passageway with the kitchen
opening off to one side of it.

I heard a man's voice answer hers as I eased the screen
closed behind me without letting it bang. That disappointed

me for a minute because I knew she must have some deliv-
eryman or collector in there with her, and I wasn't going to
put my hands over her eyes in front of some grocery clerk
or gas inspector and make a sap out of myself.

But I hated to give the harmless little plan up, so I decided to wait out there for a minute until he left, and motion
him on his way out not to give me away. Then go ahead in
and surprise her. A case of arrested development, I was!

She was saying, but very quietly, "No, I'm not going to
give you the whole thing now. You've got seventy-five, you
get the rest afterwards—"

I whistled silently and got worried. "Whew! She must
have let our grocery bills ride for over a year, to amount to
that much!" Then I decided she must be talking in cents, not
dollars.

"If I give you the whole two hundred fifty before time,
how do I know you won't haul your freight out of town—
and not do it? What comeback would I have? We're not using I.O.U.'s in this, buddy, don't forget!"

She sounded a lot tougher than I'd ever heard her before,
although she'd never exactly been a shrinking violet. But it
was his next remark that nearly dropped me where I was.
"All right, have it your way. Splash me out another cuppa
java—" And a chair hitched forward. Why, that was no de-
livery-man; he was sitting down in there and she was feeding
him!

"Better inhale it fast," she said crisply, "he'll be showing
up in another half-hour."

My first thought, of course, was what anyone else's would
have been—that it was a two-time act. But when I craned
my neck cautiously around the door just far enough to get
the back of his head in line with my eyes, I saw that was out,
too. Whatever he was and whatever he was doing there in
my house, he was no back-door John!

He had a three days' growth of beard on his jawline and
his hair ended in little feathers all over his neck, and if you'd
have whistled at his clothes they'd have probably walked off

him of their own accord and headed your way.

He looked like a stumblebum or derelict she'd hauled in out of the woods.

The next words out of her mouth, lightning fizzled around me and seemed to split my brain three ways. "Better do it right here in the house. I can't get him to go out there in the woods—he's scared of his own shadow, and you might miss him in the dark. Keep your eye on this kitchen-shade from outside. It'll be up until eight thirty.

"When you see it go down to the bottom, that means I'm leaving the house for the movies. I'll fix this back door so you can get in when I leave, too. Now, I've shown you where the phone is—right through that long hall out there. Wait'll you hear it ring before you do anything; that'll be me phoning him from the picture-house, pretending I've for-gotten something, and that'll place him for you. You'll know just where to find him, won't run into him unexpectedly on your way in.

"His back'll be toward you and I'll be distracting his at-tention over the wire. Make sure he's not still ticking when you light out, so don't spare the trigger; no one'll hear it way out here at that hour!

"I'll hear the shot over the wire and I'll hang up, but I'm sitting the rest of the show out. I wanna lose a handkerchief or something at the end and turn the theater inside out, to place myself. That gives you two hours to fade too, so I don't start the screaming act till I get back at eleven and find him——"

He said, "Where does the other hundred-seventy-five come in? Y' don't expect me to show up here afterwards and colleck, do ya?"

I heard her laugh, kind of. "It's gonna be in the one place where you can't get at it without doing what you're sup-posed to! That way I'm going to be sure you don't welsh on me! It's going to be right in his own inside coat-pocket, without his knowing it! I'm going to slip it in when I kiss him good-bye, and I know him, he'll never find it. Just reach in when you're finished with him, and you'll find it there waiting for you!"

"Lady," he whispered. "I gotta hand it to you!"

"Get going," she commanded.

I think it was that last part of it that made me see red and go off my nut, that business about slipping the blood-money right into my own pocket while I was still alive, for him to collect after I was dead. Because what I did right then certainly wasn't in character. Ben Cook, the Ben Cook of up until that minute, would have turned and sneaked out of that house unless his knees had given way first and run for his life and never showed up near there again. But I wasn't Ben Cook any more—something seemed to blow up inside me. I heard the package of candy hit the floor next to me with a smack, and then I was lurching in on them, bellowing like a goaded bull. Just rumbling sounds, more than words. "You murderess! Your—own—husband!" No, it certainly wasn't me; it was a man that neither of us had known existed until now. Evil rampant, a kind of living nemesis sprung from their own fetid plotting, like a jack-in-the-box.

There was a red-and-white checked tablecloth on the kitchen table. There was a cup and saucer on it, and a gun. I didn't see any of those things. The whole room for that matter was red, like an undeveloped photographic print.

The gun came clear, stood out, only after his arm had clamped down on it like an indicator pointing it out. My own did the same thing instinctively, but a second too late; my hand came down on his wrist instead of the gun. The crash of a pair of toppled chairs in the background was inconsequential, as was her belated shriek of baffled fury: "Give it to him now, you! Give it to him quick—or we're sunk!" Whatever else there was in that hell-howl, there wasn't fear. Any other woman would have fainted dead away; you don't know Thelma.

The cry, though, was like cause and effect; he didn't need to be told. The gun was already being lifted bodily between us, by the two pressures counteracting each other—mine pushing it away from me, his pushing it toward me. Neither of us trying to push it up, but up it went in an arc, first way over our heads, then down again to body-level once more. Outside of our flailing left arms, which had each fastened on the other's, I don't recall that our legs or the rest of our bodies moved much at all.

She could have turned the scales by attacking me herself with something, from behind. It was the one thing she didn't do—why, I don't know. Subconsciously unwilling to the last, maybe, to raise a hand to me in person.

After about thirty seconds, not more—but it seemed like an age—it finally went off. Just past my own face, over my shoulder, and out somewhere into the passageway behind us. Then it started turning slowly between us, desperately slowly, by quarter-inches, and the second time it went off it had already traveled a quarter of the compass around. It hit the side-wall, that time, broadside to the two of us. It went on past that point, turning laboriously in its double grip, and the third time it went off right into his mouth.

He took it down with him—it was his hand that had been next to it, not mine—and I just stood there with both arms out—and empty.

I suppose I would have given it to her next if it had stayed in my own hand. She expected me to; she didn't ask for mercy. "All right, I'm next!" she breathed. "Get it over as quick as you can!" And threw up both forearms horizontally in front of her eyes.

I was too tired for a minute to reach down and get it. That was what saved her. I don't remember the next few minutes after that. I was sitting slumped in one of the chairs. I must have uprighted it again, and she was saying: "The ten grand is yours now, Cookie, if you'll use your head."

The way it sounded she must have been talking for several minutes, talking herself out of what was rightfully coming to her. What she'd been saying until then hadn't registered with me, but that did.

"Get out," I said dully. "Don't hang around me. I may

change my mind yet." But the time for that was over, and she probably knew it as well as I did. The room had come back to its regular colors by now. Only the tablecloth was red any more; that and a little trickle that had come out of his open mouth onto the linoleum.

She pointed at him. "That's you, down there. Don't you get it? Readymade." She came a little closer, leaning across the table toward me on the heels of her hands. "Why pass a break like this up, Cookie? Made-to-order. Ten grand. Play ball with me, Cookie." Her voice was a purr, honey-low.

"Get ou——" I started to mutter, but my voice was lower now too. She was under my skin and working deeper down every minute. I was wide open to anything anyway, after what had happened.

She held up her hand quickly, tuning out my half-hearted protest. "All right, you caught me red-handed. You don't hear me denying it, do you? You don't see me trying to bellyache out of it, do you? It muffed, and the best man won. That's giving it to you straight from the shoulder. But the policy I slapped on you still holds good, the ten gees is yours for the taking——" She pointed down again. "And there's your corpse."

I turned my head and looked at him, kept staring thoughtfully without a word. She kept turning them out fast as her tongue could manage.

"It's up to you. You can go out to the phone and turn me in, send me up for ten years—and spend the rest of your life straightening the pants on guys at thirty per week. Have it that way if you want to. Or you can come into ten thousand dollars just by being a little smart. The guy is dead anyway, Cookie. You couldn't bring him back now even if you wanted to. What's the difference under what name he goes six-feet-under? He even gets a better break, at that; gets a buggy-ride and a lot of flowers instead of taking a dive head-first into Potter's Field!"

I hadn't taken my eyes off him, but I already wanted to hear more. "It's wacky; you're talking through your lid," I said hopefully. "How you gonna get away with it? What about all the people in this town that know me? What about the guy that sold me the insurance? What about the bench down at the store where I work? I no more look like him than—"

"If it's his face got you stopped, we can take care of that easy. And outside of a phiz, what's so different between one guy and the next? Stretch out a minute, lie down next to him—I wanna see something."

I wasn't hypocritical enough to hesitate any more. She already knew I was with her anyway—she could tell. I got down flat on the floor alongside him, shoulder to shoulder. He wasn't laid out straight by any means, but she attended to that with a few deft hitches. She stood back and measured us with her eyes. "You're about an inch taller, but the hell with that." I got up again.

She went over and pulled down the shade to the bottom, came back with cigarette-smoke boiling out of her nose. "It's a suicide, of course, otherwise the police'll stick their noses into it too heavy. A farewell note from you to me ought to hold them. Run up and bring down one of your other suits, and a complete set of everything—down to shorts and socks."

"But what're we going to do about his map?"

"A bucketful of boiling lye will take care of that. We got some down the basement, haven't we? Come on, help me get him down there."

"Where does it figure, though? You want 'em to believe he had guts enough to stick his face in that?"

"You went down there and bumped yourself through the front teeth with the gun, see? You keeled over backwards and dumped this bucket on top of your face in falling. A couple of hours under that and he'll be down to rock bottom above the shoulders; they won't have much to go by. His hair's pretty much the color of yours, and you haven't been to a dentist in years, so they can't check you in that way."

"It's still full of holes," I said.

"Sure it is," Thelma agreed, "but what reason'll they have to go looking for 'em, with me there screaming the eardums off 'em that you were my husband? And waving your good-bye note in their faces! There won't be anyone missing from this town. He was a vagrant on his way through. This was the first house he hit for a hand-out when he came out of the woods. He told me so himself, and he never got past here. The police'll be the least of our worries, when it comes to it, and as for the insurance investigator, once I get past the first hurdle I know just what to do so there's no chance for it to backfire: send him to the crematorium in a couple of days instead of planting him in the cemetery. Fat lot of good an order for an exhumation'll do them after that!"

I said about the same thing he'd said, this dead guy, only a little while ago. "You're good—damn your soul! I think we can pull it at that!"

"Think? I know we can!" She snapped her cigarette butt at the side of his face—and hit it! "Always remember—if you can get away with anything, it's worth doing. Now let's go—we haven't got much time."

I picked him up by the shoulders and she took him by the feet, and we carried him out of the kitchen and down the cellar stairs and laid him down temporarily on the floor there, any old way. The gun had gone right with him the whole way, at the end of his dangling arm.

The laundry was down there, and the oil-burner, and lines for hanging up clothes, and so on. There was a gas-heater for boiling up wash. She lit that, then she filled a pail half-full of water and put it on to heat. Then she dumped lye into it for all she was worth until there wasn't any more left around. "As long as it takes the skin off his face," she re-marked. "Go up and get the clothes now, like I told you, and doctor up a suicide-note. Better take something and get those slugs out of the kitchen-wall; it went off twice, didn't it, before it rang the bell? Rub ashes in the nicks, so they won't look new. Let me know when you're ready."

But I wasn't Ben Cook the slough any more. "And leave you alone down here with that gun? It's still got three in it. You're so full of bright ideas, how do I know you won't go back to your original parlay after all?"

She threw up her hands impatiently. "Forget it, will you! It's got to stay in his mitt like it is; you can't take it up with you. We're both in this together, aren't we? We either trust each other the whole way, or we may as well call it quits right now!"

She was blazing with an unholy sort of enthusiasm. I could tell by looking at her I had nothing to worry about as far as she was concerned any more. It was contagious, too; that was the worst part of it—greenback-fever. I turned around and beat it upstairs to the top floor. There were spots in front of my eyes, ten-spots.

I got him out a complete set of everything. For an artistic finishing-touch I even threw in a spare truss like I wore. That had figured in my examination for the insurance. I took a razor with me and a pair of clippers that I'd been in the habit of using to save myself the price of a haircut. I chased down to the desk in the living-room, got out paper, and wrote:

Thelma my darling:
I've thought it over and I guess you're right. I'll never amount to anything. I haven't had the courage to tell you yet, but Grierson turned me down last month when I asked him for a raise. I'm just a millstone around your neck, just deadweight; you'll be better off without me. When you come home tonight and read this and go looking for me, you'll know what I'm driving at. Don't go near the basement, honey; that's where I'll be. Goodby and God bless you.
Ben

Which I thought was pretty good. She did too, when I went down and showed it to her. She flashed me a look. "I think I've been underestimating you all these years."

Clouds of steam were coming from the pail of lye. "Beat it up and attend to the bullet-holes, and the blood on the kitchen-floor," I said, "while I go to work on him—"

I could hear her footsteps pattering busily back and forth over my head while I was busy down there.

I gave him a quick once-over with the razor and a cake of yellow laundry soap, clipped his neck a little, so we wouldn't have to count too much on the lye.

I piled his own worm-eaten duds into a bundle and tied it up, then outfitted him from head to foot.

It took plenty of maneuvering to slip his arm through the sleeves of the shirt and jacket without dislodging the gun from his hand.

I tied his tie and shoelaces for him as if I were his valet, and filled his pockets with all the junk I had in my own, down to the crumpled pack of butts I was toting. I strapped my wristwatch on him, and then I straightened up and gave him the once-over. He looked a lot more like me now than he had before I'd begun.

She came trooping down again, with her hat on for the movies. "Slick," she breathed. "Everything's all set upstairs. Here's the two wild bullets. What're you doing with his stuff, putting it in the furnace?"

"Nothing doing." I said. "That's muffed too often. All they need's a button or a strand of hair left over in there and we go boom! I'm taking it with me when I go and I am getting rid of it someplace else."

"That's the ticket!" she agreed. She handed me a pair of smoked glasses and an old golf cap. "Here, I dug these up for you, for when you light out. Anyone that knows you will know you anyway—but in case anyone passes you while you're on the lam, they'll do.

"Steer clear of downtown whatever you do. Better powder about ten minutes after I do; take the back door, cut through the woods; stay away from the highway until you get over to Ferndale—somebody might spot you from a passing car. You can hop a bus there at midnight—to wher-

ever you decide to hole in, and better make it the other side
of the State-line. Now we gotta finish up fast. I phoned the
drug store to send over some aspirin, told 'em you felt kinda
low—"

"What's the idea?"

"Don't you get it? I'm leavin' just as the errand-boy gets
here; he even sees you kiss me good-bye at the front door.
Hold him up a minute hunting for change, so that he has me
walking in front of him down the street toward the show. I
don't want to get the chair for something I didn't do,
Cookie! Now, what name are you going to use and where'll I
reach you when the pay-off comes through?"

I laughed harshly. "You're pretty anxious to see that I get
my cut."

"I'm glad you used that word," she said drily. "It's my
favorite little word. Nuts! You can't come back here; you
know that! I've gotta get it to you. What're you worrying
about? We've got each other stopped, haven't we? If I try to
hog the dough, all you do is show up, it goes back where it
came from, and we both land in clink. On the other hand,
you can't get it without little Thelma—"

"We split it seventy-five, twenty-five, and little Thelma's
on the short end for being such a smart girl," I growled.

Something gave one corner of her mouth a little hike up.
"Done," she said. "Now hurry up, give him his facial. Meas-
ure the distance off."

We stood him upright on his feet, then let him down
backwards in a straight line toward the heater on which the
pail of lye was sizzling. The back of his head cleared it by
two, three inches.

"Move him in a little closer." she said. "His conk's supposed to tip it over as he goes down."

"All right, stand back," I said, "and watch your feet."

I took it off the stove, turned it upside down, and doused
it on him, arched as far away from the splash as I could get.
It dropped down on his head like a mold; only a little spat-
tered on his body below the shoulders. Just as the pail

dropped over his head like a visor, the front doorbell rang.

The last thing she said as she went hustling up was, "Watch out where you step—don't leave any tracks!"

I caught up with her halfway down the front hall. "Whoa! Pass over that hundred-seventy-five you were going to stuff into my pocket. I can't live on air the next few weeks!"

She took it grudgingly out of her handbag. "It comes off your share, don't forget," she let me know.

"All right, and here's one for your memory-book," I whispered. "I'm Ned Baker at the Marquette Hotel over in Middleburg. Don't put it on paper, but see that you hang onto it. It's easy enough—Cook, Baker, see?"

The bell rang a second time.

"About three weeks, the minute I put the check through," she promised. "All set? Here goes! Loosen your tie—you're staying in and you're in a hari-kari mood. Play up!"

I stayed where I was. She went to the door squalling, "G'by, hon! Sure you won't change your mind and come with me?" She opened the door and an eighteen-year-old kid named Larry whom we both knew by sight said, "Package from the drug store, Mrs. Cook. Thirty-five cents."

Again she shook the house to the rafters. "Here's your aspirin, dear!"

I shuffled up acting like a sick calf. I separated one of the tens she'd just given me from the rest and offered it to him. He said he didn't have that much change. "Wait a minute, I think I've got it inside," I said. Meanwhile, she was sticking her snoot up at me. "G'by, dear. You won't be lonely now, will you?"

He was facing my way, so I tried to look tragic. "Enjoy your show," I murmured bravely, pecking at her with my mouth. I walked down the steps with her and part of the way toward the sidewalk, with my arm around her waist. She turned back to wave a couple times, and I waved back at her. The kid was taking it all in from the doorway.

"They got a revival of Garbo tonight," he remarked when

I came back. "Don't you like Garbo, Mr. Cook?"

I sighed. "I got too much on my mind tonight, Larry," I told him. I let her get to the first crossing, then I brought out the thirty-five cents and gave him a dime for himself. He thanked me and started off after her.

I locked the door (she had her own key) and then I bolted back to the cellar-stairs and took a last look down from the head of them. Threads of steam were still coming out from under the rim of the lye-pail, upturned there over his face.

I picked up his bundle of clothes, which I'd left at the top of the stairs, and wrapped them in good strong brown paper. The two bullets were in there with them, and the scrapings from his jaw and neck on scraps of paper. The brownish rag, too, with which she'd scoured the little blood off the linoleum.

The latter didn't have a mark left on it to the naked eye— and there was no reason for them to give it a benzidine test. The bullet-holes were okay too; she'd spread them to look like knotholes in the wood and dirtied them with ashes. She'd even washed and put away the used coffee-cup, and the note was in place on the desk.

I left my own hat up on the rack, and put on the cap, pulled it well down over my eyes.

I left the lights just the way they were in all the rooms, then I went up to the rear room on the second floor, which was dark, and stood watching for a long time. There weren't any houses in back of us, just a big open field with the woods off to the right.

In the daytime, crossing the field to get to them, I might have been spotted from one of the houses farther down, but not at this hour. It was a clear night, but there wasn't any moon.

I went downstairs, opened the screen-door, pulled the wooden one closed behind me, let the screen one flap back in place, and jumped away in a hurry from the square of light that still came through the oblong pane in the wooden one. We would have locked that on the inside if we had both left the house together, but staying home alone the way I was supposed to tonight, it could very well stay unlocked without arousing suspicion.

I cut diagonally away from the house, to get out of sight of the roadway that fronted it and bisected the woods all the way to Ferndale. It took a turn, however, halfway between the two points, so going through the woods was really a short-cut.

Within five minutes after I had left the kitchen-door, and less than a quarter of an hour since Thelma had left the house all told, the first skinny saplings closed around me and hid me from sight.

By a quarter to twelve the trees were starting to thin out again, this time in front of me, and the lights of Ferndale were glimmering through them. I was half-shot and my feet were burning, but it was worth it; I hadn't seen a living soul—and what was more important, not a living soul had seen me. I'd kept from getting lost and going around in a circle, which could have happened to me quite easily in those woods, by always managing to keep the highway to Ferndale parallel with me on my right. Even when I was out of sight of it, an occasional car whizzing by gave it away to me. Otherwise, I might very well have done a Babe-in-the-Woods act and come out again where I started from. I'd opened the parcel and retied it again on my way. Took out the two slugs and the bloody rag and buried them in three separate places.

The clothes themselves were too bulky to bury with my bare fingernails, and I wasn't just going to leave them under a stone or anything. Nor could I risk putting a match to them and burning them—the light might have given me away to someone. The safest thing was to keep them with me and get rid of them long afterwards at my leisure.

Ferndale wasn't much more than a crossroads, but the interstate buses stopped there. I stopped for a minute and brushed myself off as well as I could before I showed out in the open. I looked respectable enough, but that was almost a drawback in itself.

A well-dressed guy dropping down out of nowhere at midnight to board a bus, without a through ticket, wasn't really the most unnoticeable thing in the world. But I had no choice in the matter. Nor very much time to make up my mind. The last one through was sometime between twelve and one. I decided, however, not to buy a Middleburg ticket from here but ride right through past it to the end of the line, and then double back to Middleburg from that end in a couple of days. That would make the trail a little harder to pick up—just in case.

As for the sun-glasses, which I'd been carrying in my pocket, I decided against them altogether. That was the one detail, it seemed to me, about which Thelma hadn't shown very good judgment. No one in Ferndale knew me in the first place, and they'd only attract attention instead of lessening it. People don't wear those things in the middle of the night, no matter how weak their eyes are supposed to be.

I straightened my shoulders and strolled casually out of the trees into the open, past an outlying cottage or two, dead to the world at this hour, and onto the single stretch of paved sidewalk that Ferndale boasted. A quick-lunch place was open and blazing with light, and the bus depot was down at the far end. There was a small but up-to-date little waiting-room there, washrooms, a magazine-stand, etc. No one around but the colored porter and an elderly man who looked like he was waiting to meet somebody getting off the incoming bus.

I went up to the ticket-window as casually as I could and rapped on the counter a couple of times. Finally the porter called out, "Johnson! Somebody at the wicket!" and the ticket-seller came out of the back someplace.

I said, "Gimme a through ticket to Jefferson." That was the neighboring state capital, terminus of this line.

He said, "I don't know if I can get you a seat at this hour; usually pretty full up. You shoulda put in a reservation ahead— There's a six-o'clock bus, though."

"Lissen," I said, looking him in the eye, "I gotta get home. Whaddya think I'm going to do, sit around here all night waiting for the morning bus?"

He called over my shoulder to the elderly gent, who was reading a paper, "You meeting somebody on the next bus, mister?"

The old fellow said, "Yep, my nevvew's coming down on it—"

"That's that, then," he said to me indifferently. "'Leven eighty."

"When's it get in?" I asked, pocketing my change.

"Ten minutes," he said, and went back inside again.

I was down at the quick-lunch filling up on hot dogs when the bus slithered in. I picked up my package and went up toward it. A young fellow of high-school age was getting off and being greeted by the elderly gent. I showed my ticket and got on.

Its lights were off and most of the passengers were sprawled out asleep. The ticket-seller had been right: there was only a single vacant seat in the whole conveyance, the one that the kid had just got out of! It was a bum one on the aisle, too.

My seat-mate, by the window, had his hat down over his nose and was breathing through his mouth. I didn't pay any attention to him, reached up and shoved my bundle onto the rack overhead, sat back and relaxed. The driver got on again, the door closed, and we started off with a lurch.

My lightweight bundle hadn't been shoved in far enough in the dark: the motion of the bus promptly dislodged it and it toppled down across the thighs of the man next to me. He came to with a nervous start and grunted from under his hat-brim.

"Excuse me," I said, "didn't mean to wake you—"

He shoved his hat back and looked at me. "Why, hullo, Cook!" he said. "Where you going at this hour of the night?" And held his hand spaded at me.

A couple of years went by, with my face pointed straight ahead and ice-water circulating in my veins. There wasn't very much choice of what to do about it. Even if the bus had still been standing still with its door open, which it wasn't any more, it wouldn't have done any good to jump off it. He'd already seen me.

And to try to pass the buck and tell him to his face he had the wrong party, well what chance had I of getting away with that, with our shoulders touching, even though it was dark inside the bus? I couldn't stop it from getting light in a few hours, and there wasn't any other seat on the bus. All I'd succeed in doing would be snubbing him, offending him, and making him start thinking there must be something phony afoot; in other words, indelibly impressing the incident upon his memory.

Whereas if I took it in my stride, lightly, maybe I could keep it from sinking in too deeply; maybe I could do something about the timing to blur it a little, make him think later on that it was the night before and not tonight that he'd ridden with me on a bus. It had to be the night before; it couldn't be the same night that I was supposed to be bumping myself off down in the cellar back at Copeland Drive!

"Well, for the luvva Pete, Sherrill!" I said with shaky cordiality. "Where you going yourself at this hour of the night?" I shook his mitt, but there was less pressure now on his side than mine.

"Y'acted like y'didn't know me for a minute," he complained, but rapidly thawed out again. "What'd you get on way the hell out at Ferndale for?" he said.

But that one had to be squelched at all costs, no matter how unconvincing it sounded. After all, he'd definitely been asleep when they pulled into Ferndale, he couldn't have seen who got on there.

"I didn't. What's the matter with *you*?" I said in surprise. "I changed seats, come back here from up front, that's all." There was a little girl holding one of the front seats in her own right, but she was asleep with her head on her mother's lap; it looked like the seat was vacant from where we were. "He'll forget about it by the time she straightens up in the morning—let's hope," I thought.

He seemed to forget it then and there. "Funny I missed seeing you when I got on," was all he said. "I was the last one in; they even held it for me a minute—" He offered me a cigarette, took one himself, seemed to have no more use for sleep. "Where you heading for, anyway?" he asked.

"Jefferson, I said."

"That's funny," he said, "I am too!"

If he could have heard the things I was saying inside myself about him at the moment, he would have let out a yell and probably dived through the window, glass and all. "How come?" I said, between unheard swear-words.

I knew it would be my turn right after his, and I was so busy shaping up my own explanation, I only half-heard his. Something about the manager phoning him at the last minute after he'd already gone home that afternoon, to pinch-hit for our store's buyer, who'd been laid up with the flu, and look after some consignments of neckties that were waiting down there and badly needed in stock. "What's taking you down there?" he asked, as I knew he would.

I told him I had to see a specialist, that I'd been below par for some time and none of the docs back home had seemed able to do a thing for me.

"When you going back?" he wanted to know.

"'Morrow afternoon," I said. "Be home in time for supper—" I had to be "back" by then; I couldn't hope to fog him on the time element by more than twenty-four hours. That I'd even be able to do that much was highly doubtful, but I might just get away with it.

"That's just about when I'll be going back, too," he said chummily. "Be back at work Friday morning."

I answered with careful emphasis: "Whaddya mean, Friday? The day after tomorrow'll be Thursday. Tonight's Tuesday."

"No," he said innocently, "you've got your dates mixed.

Tonight's Wednesday."

This went on for about five minutes between us, without heat of course. I finally pulled my horns in when he offered: "Wait, I'll ask the driver, he ought to be able to straighten us out—"

"Never mind, guess you're right," I capitulated. I wasn't keen on attracting the driver's attention to myself in any shape, form, or manner. But I'd done what I wanted to: I'd succeeded in conditioning Sherill's mind. Later he wouldn't be sure whether it *was* Wednesday or not, when he thought back to tonight.

Right on top of that came a honey. "Whaddya say we split expenses while we're there?" he offered. "Share the same hotel room."

"What do I need a hotel room for?" I said shortly. "I told you I'm going back on the afternoon bus!"

"Hell," he said, "if you're as rundown as you say you are, funny you should be willing to go without sleep a whole night! We don't get into Jefferson till seven. You got a before-breakfast appointment with your doctor?"

The skepticism in his voice had to be nipped before it got steam up, I could see; the only way seemed to be by falling in with his suggestion. I could let him start back alone, pretend my appointment had been postponed until afternoon and I had to take a later bus. Technically, even one of those could get me home in time for my own suicide.

We had our breakfasts together at the bus depot and then we checked in at a hotel down the street called the Jefferson. I let him sign first, and stalled shaking a clot out of the pen until he'd already started toward the elevator. Then I wrote "Ned Baker" under his name, "Frisco." That was far enough away—a big enough place to assure anonymity. I'd met him en route; that was all. I wasn't going to do it to him right here in this hotel, anyway, and there was no earthly reason for him to take another look at that register in checking out, nor for the clerk to mention me by name in his presence; we'd paid in advance on account of our scarcity of baggage.

He asked for a ten-thirty call and hung a "Do not disturb" on the door when we got up to the room. Then we turned in, one to a bed. "I'm dead," was the last thing he yawned.

"You betcha sweet life you are, brother!" I thought grimly. He dropped off into a deep, dreamless sleep—his last one. I knew I was safe enough while I had him right with me, and until he got ready to start back; I wasn't going to do it in this hotel room anyway. So I just lay there on my back staring up at the ceiling, waiting, waiting. The wings of the death-angel were spread over us in that room; there was the silence of the grave.

The phone-peal, when it came, shattered it like a bomb. I felt good, because the time was drawing shorter now. This new self of mine seemed to be agreeing with me. "Toss you for the shower," I offered.

"Go ahead," he stretched, "I like to take my time."

It was a little thing like that changed my plans, brought it on him even quicker. Just before I turned on the water I heard him open and close the door. He called in, "Gee, pretty liberal! They hand you a morning paper compliments of the management in this place!"

When I came out he was sitting there on the bed with it spread out alongside him. He wasn't looking at it, he was looking at me; he was holding his head as though he'd been waiting for me to show up in the bathroom doorway. There were three white things there on that bed, but it was his face that was whiter even than the pillows or the paper.

"What're you looking at me like that for?" I said gruffly, and then my own got white too.

He began shrinking away from me along the edge of the bed. He said: "They found your body in the cellar of your house—last night at eleven—you committed suicide. It's here, on the first page of this Jefferson paper—"

I dropped the towel and picked the paper up, but I didn't look at it; I was watching him over the top of it. He was shaking all over. He said, "Who—was that? Who'd you do it to?"

"This is a mistake," I said furrily. "They've got me mixed up with somebody else. Somebody by the same name, maybe—"

His back was arched against the headboard of the bed by now, as if he couldn't get far enough away from me. He said, "But that's your address there—25 Copeland Drive—I know your address! It even tells about your working for the store—it gives your wife's name, Thelma—it tells how she found your body, with your face all eaten away with lye—" I could see beads of sweat standing out in a straight line across his forehead. "Who was that, Cook? It must have been—somebody! My God, did *you*—?"

I said, "Well, look at me! You see me here with you, dontcha? You can see it's not me, cantcha?" But that wasn't what he was driving at, and I knew it as well as he did. He knew I was alive, all right; what he wanted to know was who was dead.

I don't know what the outcome would have been, if he hadn't given himself away by starting to dress in that frightened, jerky way—snatching at his clothes as if he was afraid of me, trying to stay as far out of my way as he could while he struggled getting his things on. I suppose it would have happened anyway, before I would have let him go back to our own town, knowing what he now did. But not right then, not right there.

I told myself, coldly, as I watched him fumbling, panting, sweating to get into his things in the least possible time, "He's going straight out of here and give me away! It's written all over him. He won't even wait till he gets back to-night—phone them long distance right from here, or else tip the cops off right here in Jefferson. Well—he's not going to get out that door!"

The phone was between the two beds. He was bent over on the outside of his, which was nearer the door, struggling with his laces. What was holding him up was that in his frenzied haste he'd snarled them up into a knot. The door didn't worry me as much as the phone. I moved around, naked, into the aisle between the two beds, cutting him off from it.

"Why all the rush?" I asked.

"I gotta hustle and get after those ties," he said in a muffled voice. He couldn't bring himself to look around at me, rigidly kept his head turned the other way.

I moved up closer behind him. My shadow sort of fell across him, cutting off the light from the window. "And what're you going to do about what you just read in the paper?"

"Why, nothing," he faltered. "I—I guess like you said, it's just some kind of mistake—" His voice cracked into a placating little laugh; you wouldn't have known what it was by the sound of it, though. And the last thing he ever said was to repeat, "Nothing—nothing at all, really."

"You're blamed tooting you're not," I rasped. I don't know if he even heard me. I suddenly pulled him down flat on his back, by the shoulders, from behind. I had a last flash of his face, appalled, eyes rolling, staring up at mine. Then the two pillows were over it, soft, yielding, and I was pressing them down with my whole weight.

Most of the struggle, of course, was in his legs, which had been hanging down free over the side of the bed. They jolted upward to an incredible height at first, far higher than his head, then sank all the way back to the floor again, and after that kept teetering upward and downward like a seesaw between bed-level and the floor.

It was the very fact that they were loose like that that prevented his throwing me off him. He was off-balance, the bed ended just under his hips, and he couldn't get a grip on the floor with his heels. As for his arms, they were foreshortened by the pressure of the big pillows like a bandage. He only had the use of them below the elbows, couldn't double them back on themselves far enough to get at my face, claw as he might. I kept my face and neck arched back just beyond their reach, holding the pillows down by my abdomen in the center and by the pressure of my shoulders and splayed arms on each end.

The bedsprings groaned warningly once or twice of approaching doom. Outside of that there wasn't a sound in the room but my own breathing.

The leg-motion was the best possible barometer. It quickened to an almost frenzied lashing as suffocation set in, then slowed to a series of spasmodic jerks that would slacken inevitably to a point of complete motionlessness. Just before it had been reached, I suddenly reared back and flung the pillows off, one each way. His face was contorted to the bursting-point, his eyes glazed and sightless, but the fingers of his upturned hands were still opening and closing convulsively, grabbing at nothing; he was unmistakably still alive, but whether he could come back again or would succumb anyway in a minute or two more was the question. It was important to me to beat his heart to the final count.

I dragged him off the bed, around the second bed, and got him over to the window. I hoisted him up, turned him toward it, and balanced him lightly with one arm against my side, as if I was trying to revive him. I looked, and I looked good. The room was on the fourteenth floor, and we'd taken one of the cheaper ones; it gave onto an air-shaft, not the street. There were, probably, windows all the way down, under this one—but the point was, there weren't any *opposite;* that side was blank. No one could look in here.

I think he would have pulled through; he was beginning to revive as air got into his lungs. The congested blood started leaving his face little by little, his eyes closed instead of staying wide open, but you could hear him breathing again, hoarsely. So I edged him a little closer, threw up the lower sash all the way to the top—and just stepped back from him. I didn't touch him, just took my support away, retreated farther into the room. He wavered there, upright by the open window. Vertigo had evidently set in as his lungs began to function and his heartbeat came back to normal. It was a toss-up whether he'd go back, forward, or sideways; the only sure thing was he wasn't staying on his own feet just then, and was going into a faint.

Maybe there was some kind of a draught pulling at him from the long, deep shaft out there; I don't know. He went forward—as though a current of air were sucking him through the window. It was a good high window. His head just missed the sash bisecting it. He folded up at the waist across the ledge, half in, half out, like a lazy guy leaning too far out in slow motion—and gravity did the rest. Death beat his glimmering faculties to the punch—he was gone before he could fling up his arms, grab at anything. His legs whipped after him like the tail of a kite—and the window-square was empty.

The impact seemed to come up long afterwards, from far away, muffled, distant, and even the new me didn't like the sound of it very well. I didn't make the mistake of going closer and looking down after him. Almost immediately there was the sound of another window being thrown up somewhere down the line, a pause, and then a woman's screech came tearing up the shaft.

I saw that one of his unlaced shoes had come off while I was hauling him across the room. I edged it back under his own bed, smoothed that from a condition of having been struggled upon back to a condition of just having been slept in, particularly the pillows. I erased a blurred line across the carpet-nap that his one dragging shoe had made, with the flat of my own shoe.

Then I picked up the towel I'd already wet once, went back into the bathroom, turned on the shower full-blast, and got back under it again. Its roar deadened everything, but a sudden draft on my wet shoulder tipped me off when they'd used the passkey on the room-door. "Hey, Sherrill!" I boomed out just as they came in, "can I borrow some of your shaving-cream?" I stuck my head farther out and hollered, "What's the matter with ya, didya go back to sleep in there? That's the third time I've asked ya the same question—"

Then I saw them all standing looking in at me. "What's up?" I yelled, and reached out and shut off the water.

The sudden silence was stunning.

The hotel detective said, "Your roommate just fell out of the window in there."

"Oh, my God!" I gasped, and had to hang onto the rubber curtain to keep from tipping over, myself, for a minute. Some soap got in my eyes and made them fill with water. Through it I could see them all looking at me, from the bellhop up, as though they knew how bad I felt, and felt sorry for me.

Three weeks to the day, after that morning in the hotel at Jefferson, Thelma's message was waiting for me in my mailbox at the Marquette in Middleburg. I had been holed-up there for two weeks past, from the moment I'd felt it prudent to leave Jefferson. Not that I'd been under arrest or even suspicion at any time, but the detectives there had, naturally, questioned me about how well I'd known Sherrill, whether he'd said anything to indicate he intended suicide. I seemed to satisfy them on all points.

They kept me waiting another twenty-four hours—and on pins and needles. Then they sent word that I was free to leave whenever I wanted to. I didn't waste time hanging around once I heard that! It struck me that I hadn't been called on to make a deposition at any coroner's inquest, but I wasn't inclined to argue with them on that point. Nor did I bother trying to find out what disposition had been made of Sherrill's remains. I simply left—while the leaving was good!

Beautifully as I'd got away with that, though, I had plenty of other things to get jittery about while I was waiting to hear from her the next couple weeks in Middleburg. I kept wondering whether she was going to double-cross me or not, and the suspense got worse day by day and hour by hour. If she did, I had no come-back.

She'd soaped me up by saying all I had to do if she tried

to hold out was show up home and give her away. True enough as far as it went, but there was one thing I'd overlooked at the time: what was to keep her there on tap once she got her paws on the insurance check? All she had to do was blow out in some other direction and—good-bye ten grand!

That was what really had me down, the knowledge that she had been holding a trump-hand all through this little game of ours—with me trying to bluff her. And from what I knew of her, she didn't bluff easy. I'd even set a deadline in my own mind: forty-eight hours more, and if I didn't hear from her, I'd head back home myself, no matter what the risk, and land on her with both feet before she took a powder out on me.

Nothing had muffed at her end—I knew that for a fact; so she couldn't alibi that she wasn't in line for the money. I'd been buying our hometown papers daily ever since I'd been in Middleburg, watching to see if the thing would curdle or start to smell bad, and it hadn't.

It would have been in headlines in a minute if it had, but all I had were the few consecutive items bearing on it that I'd clipped out and stuck away in my wallet. I'd been taking them out nightly and going over them, to reassure myself, and it was as good as television. First, the news announcement that had sent Sherrill to his death (although he'd seen it in a Jefferson, not a hometown paper).

Then an inconspicuous obituary the next day, mentioning a date for the cremation. Then a twenty-four-hour postponement of the cremation, with no reason given (this had given me a bad night, all right!). Then finally, two days later, the bare announcement that the cremation had taken place the day before. That was all, but that was plenty. The thing was signed, sealed, and delivered—we'd got away with it!

Even outside of all that, anyone in my position, naturally, would have been jittery. Just having to sit tight day by day waiting for the pay-off was reason enough. The one hundred and seventy-five dollars I'd chiseled out of her was starting to run down; I wanted to get my hands on the real dough and get out of this part of the country altogether. Middleburg, after all, wasn't so very far away from the hometown. Somebody who has known me might drop over from there and spot me when I least expected it; the young mustache I was nursing along was no guarantee at all against recognition.

I stayed in my room most of the time, let them think what I'd told Sherrill, that I was in precarious health. I began to look the part, too, so it wasn't hard to sell the idea. I haunted my letter-box downstairs, and just went as far as the corner-stand once a day, to get the hometown paper, the Kay City *Star*. I always soft-pedaled it by buying a Jefferson one and a Middleburg one along with it, and then discarding them in the nearest trash-can.

And up in my room I always tore the name and place of publication off the tops of every page of each copy, carefully burning the strips in an ashtray, so the chambermaid or anyone else finding it wouldn't know just where it was published.

I had a bad minute or two one evening when the news vendor couldn't find me a copy of the hometown rag. "They usually send me two," he apologized, "but they were one short today, and there's another gent been buying 'em right along, like you do yourself, and he musta got here ahead of you, I guess, and took the only one I had—"

I got very quiet, then finally I said off-handedly, "He a regular customer of yours? How long's he been doing that?"

"Oh, two, three weeks now—'bout as long as you have. He lives right in the same hotel you do, I think; I see him come in and go out of there a lot. Nice guy, minds his own business—"

I said, even more off-handedly than before, "D'je happen to mention to him that I been taking the Kay City *Star* from you too?"

"Nah!" he said emphatically, "I never said 'Boo' to him."

I had to be satisfied with that, and in a day or two my

apprehension had dulled again, not having anything further to feed on. The Marquette was no skyscraper honeycomb; I'd seen all the faces in it by this time, and there was definitely no one there that knew me or that I knew, or that I'd ever seen before. Nor did the register, when I went over it without much trouble, show any Kay City entries.

The whole thing was just a harmless coincidence, that was all; probably the guy took the *Star* purely for business reasons. There was a pudgy realtor who had the room across the hall from mine; I'd met him once or twice on the elevator, and it was probably he, keeping tab on real estate opportunities in various townships. That reassured me completely; he fitted the newsman's description exactly, and never even so much as looked at me the few times we happened on each other.

One night I eavesdropped while I was unlocking my own door and overheard him having a long argument with somebody over the phone. "That's an ideal site," he was saying. "Tell 'em they can't have it at that price. Why, it would be a gold-mine if we leased it for a filling-station—"

On the twenty-first morning after Sherrill's death, I stepped up to the hotel desk—and for the first time there was white showing in my letter-box! My overwrought nerves began crackling like high-tension wires. It had a Kay City postmark. In my excitement I dropped it and this real-estate guy, who had come up to the desk for his own mail just then, picked it up and handed it back to me without a word.

I went over in a corner of the lobby and tore it open. There was no signature—probably she hadn't wanted to hand me a blackjack that could be used against her—but it was from her all right. I recognized the writing, although she'd tried to distort it a little, or else her excitement had done that for her.

Jackie has come through pretty. If you want to see him, you know what to do about it. It's up to you to do the traveling, not me. I'm not at the old place any more, so it'll be okay. 10 State Street is where you'll find me.

The way I burned it's a wonder smoke didn't curl out of my ears. So it was up to me to do the traveling, was it? She knew what a chance I'd be taking by showing up home, even if she had changed addresses!

I came to a sudden decision. "All right, for being so smart, she's going to pony over the whole ten grand now! I'm going down there and clean her out! And if she opens her trap, she's going to suddenly quit being alive!"

I folded the thing up, put it in my pocket, and went out. I hit the seedy part of Jefferson, across the railroad tracks, and picked up a .32 and some cartridges at a hock-shop without too many questions asked, particularly the one about where was my license. I came back and I booked a seat on the three o'clock bus, which would get me to Kay City just after dark. I bought a cheap pair of reading glasses and a flat tin of shoe polish. I went back to my room, knocked the lenses out of their tortoise-shell rims and heavied up my mustache with a little of the blacking.

At half-past two in the afternoon I went downstairs and paid my bill and turned in my key. The clerk didn't say a word, but I saw him stick a bright-red pasteboard strip like a bookmark in my letter-box. "What's that for?" I asked idly.

"That's to show it's available."

"You've got one in the one right next to it too." I squinted.

"Yeah, 919, across the hall from you, checked out about half an hour ago too."

The only thing that kept me from getting flurried was that his check-out had come ahead of mine, and not after; otherwise, I'd have suspected there was something phony about it. But this way, how could he have possibly known I intended leaving myself, when the first warning I'd given was this very minute?

"Just the same," I said to myself, "he's been taking the Kay City *Star* every day. I'm gonna take a good look in that bus, and if he's in it, I don't get on. I'm not taking any chances, not gonna lay myself open the way I did running into Sherrill!"

I timed myself to get to the depot just five minutes ahead of starting-time. The bus was standing there waiting to go. I walked all down one side of it, gandering in every window, and then doubled back on the other side, doing the same thing, before I got on. There wasn't a sign of him.

I found my seat and sat down on the edge of it, ready to hop off if he showed at the last moment. He didn't.

I looked them all over after a while, and there wasn't anything about any of them to call for a second look. Nor did I get even a first one from anybody. It was dark by the time we hit Ferndale, and about nine thirty when we got into Kay City at the downtown terminus. I slipped on the lensless pair of rims just before the doors opened, and didn't waste any time lingering about the brightly lighted depot. Outside in the street-dusk I'd pass muster, as long as I didn't stop to stare into any glaring shop windows.

State Street was a quiet residential thoroughfare lined with prosperous residences; it was nearer in to the heart of the city than where we had lived, though. I reconnoitered number 10 from the opposite side of the street, going past it first and then doubling back. It was just a substantial brick house, two-storied, without anything about it to make me leery. Only one window, on the ground floor, showed a light. I thought, "What the hell is she doing in a place like that?" I decided she must have rented a furnished room with the family that owned it.

I crossed over farther down, and then once more started back toward it. There wasn't a soul on the street, at the moment. Instead of going right up to the door, I edged around to the window where the light was and took a look in.

Thelma was in the room there, and she seemed to be alone. She was right in a line with the window, sitting by herself in a big chair, holding a cigarette and staring intently over into a corner which I couldn't see from where I was. I could tell she was under a strain—the hand holding the cigarette shook visibly each time she lifted it. I waited a while, then I tapped lightly on the pane.

She looked square over at me, didn't show a bit of surprise. She jerked her head in the direction of the front door, but didn't get up or anything. I went around to it and tried it cautiously. She'd left it on the latch, for me to walk in without ringing. I closed it softly behind me, tapped the .32 in my pocket, and moved a few paces down the hall, listening. The house was dead; the people were out, whoever they were.

I put my hand on the side-door that led to the room where she was and pushed it open. She was still sitting there, shakily holding that cigarette. "Hello, Cookie," she said in a funny voice.

"Hello, yourself," I growled, and I looked all around the room. It was empty, of course. There was another, leading out somewhere toward the back, its door standing wide open, but I couldn't see a thing through it.

"Did you get my note?" she said. Then she said: "You've come back to kill me, of course. I've had a feeling it would end up that way all along. Is that it, in your pocket there?" And her eyes rolled around spasmodically, not at all matching the quiet dryness of her voice.

I said, "What's the matter with you, you paralyzed or something? Whaddya keep sitting there like that for? Gimme the dough, all of it!"

She said, "What was our arrangement, again?"

"Twenty-five, seventy-five, with you on the short end. But that's out, now; I'm taking the whole works—and here's the convincer—" I took the gun out slowly.

The cigarette fell, but she still didn't move.

"Up!" a voice said in my ear, and I could feel snub-nosed steel boring into my spine through my clothes. Then half of Kay City seemed to come into the room all at one time, through the door behind me and also through that other one opposite. One guy even stood up from behind the big easy chair she'd been in all along, a gun on me across her shoulder.

I let the .32 drop and showed my palms. I knew the Kay City chief of police by a picture of him I'd once seen. "Well," he purred, "nice of you to drop in at my house like this! Wrists out, please!"

I said to her, "You dirty, double-crossing——"

"I didn't cross you, Cookie," she said wearily. "They tumbled the very next day——"

"Shut up!" I raged at her.

"That's all right, Cook," the chief of police said soothingly.

"The guy was never cremated at all—we saw to that. We inserted that phony announcement in the paper ourselves. She's been in custody ever since—it's just that we were waiting for the insurance check to come through, to use in evidence. You thought you were good, didn't you? Want me to tell you what you had for breakfast Tuesday? Or what tune you whistled when you were getting ready for bed a week ago Sunday night? No trouble at all!"

They had to hold me up between them. "I didn't kill him," I gasped, "it was self-defense——"

The fat realtor from the Marquette came around in front of me. "Maybe it was self-defense when you pushed Sherrill out of the window in Jefferson?"

"I was taking a shower; I didn't have anything to do with——"

"Sherrill didn't die," he said. "A couple of clothes-lines at the bottom of that shaft were kinder to him than you were. He's been in a hospital down there with his back in a plaster-cast for the past three weeks. Crippled for life, maybe, thanks to you—but able to talk. He told us all about it, that's how it blew up at this end."

Something seemed to blow up in me too, the way it had that night. I was Ben Cook again, who'd never done anything wrong in his life. It was as if the streak of badness had worked itself out, somehow.

I shuddered and covered my face with my manacled hands. "I'm—I'm sorry. Well, you've got me, and maybe it's all for the best—I'm ready to take what's coming to me—"

"Don't worry, you're going to," said the chief of police. "Take him over to headquarters and book him. Take her back to the cooler."

As we were leaving, one of the detectives said: "All for ten grand! If you'da just hung on a little while longer, you'da gotten it without lifting your finger—like that!" He took out a cablegram from his pocket.

It was addressed to me, at the old address. It had come in only a couple days before. It was from London, from some attorney I'd never heard of. It informed me my first wife, Florence, had died two months before and left me a legacy of more than three thousand pounds.

Ten thousand dollars!

I didn't show any emotion at all. Just turned to them and asked them if they'd do me a favor.

"Give you a swift kick, I suppose," one of the detectives sneered.

"It's mine to do with as I want, isn't it, this dough? Turn it over to Sherrill, will you, for me? Maybe it'll help to get him fixed up so he can walk again."

They all looked at me in surprise, as though this was out of character, coming from me. It really wasn't, though. None of us are one hundred percent bad and none of us are one hundred percent good—we're all just kind of mixed, I guess. Maybe that's why the Judge, the Higher One, feels sorry for us. A whole row of black marks and then a single white mark at the very end. Which cancels which? I'll find out for sure pretty soon now. . . .

YOU'LL NEVER SEE ME AGAIN

It was the biscuits started it. How he wished, afterward, that she'd never made those biscuits! But she made them, and she was proud of them. Her first try. Typical bride-and-groom stuff. The gag everyone's heard for years, so old it has whiskers down to here. So old it isn't funny any more. No, it isn't funny; listen while it's told.

He wasn't in the mood for playing house. He'd been working hard all day over his drafting-board. Even if they'd been good he probably would have grunted, "Not bad," and let it go at that. But they weren't good; they were atrocious. They were as hard as gravel; they tasted like lye. She'd put in too much of something and left out too much of something else, and life was too short to fool around with them.

"Well, I don't hear you saying anything about them," she pouted.

All he said was: "Take my advice, Smiles, and get 'em at the corner bakery after this."

"That isn't very appreciative," she said. "If you think it was much fun bending over that hot oven—"

"If you think it's much fun eating them—I've got a blue-print to do tomorrow; I can't take punishment like this!"

One word led to another. By the time the meal was over, her fluffy golden head was down inside her folded arms on the table and she was making broken-hearted little noises.

Crying is an irritant to a tired man. He kept saying things he didn't want to. "I could have had a meal in any restaurant without this. I'm tired. I came home to get a little rest, not the death scene from *Camille* across the table from me."

She raised her head at that. She meant business now. "If I'm annoying you, that's easily taken care of! You want it quiet; we'll see that you *get* it quiet. No trouble at all about that."

She stormed into the bedroom and he could hear drawers slamming in and out. So she was going to walk out on him, was she? For a minute he was going to jump up and go in there after her and put his arms around her and say: "I'm sorry, Smiles; I didn't mean what I said." And that probably would have ended the incident then and there.

But he checked himself. He remembered a well-meaning piece of advice a bachelor friend of his had given him before his marriage. And bachelors always seem to know so much about marriage rules! "If she should ever threaten to walk out on you, and they all do at one time or another," this sage had counseled him, "there's only one way for you to handle that. Act as though you don't care; let her go. She'll come back fast enough, don't worry. Otherwise, if you beg her not to, she'll have the upper hand over you from then on."

He scratched himself behind one ear. "I wonder if he was right?" he muttered. "Well, the only way to find out is to try it."

So he left the table, went into the living-room, snapped on a reading-lamp, sprawled back in a chair, and opened his evening paper, perfectly unconcerned to all appearances. The only way you could tell he wasn't, was by the little glances he kept stealing over the top of the paper every once in a while to see if she was really going to carry out her threat.

She acted as if she were. She may have been waiting for him to come running in there after her and beg for forgiveness, and when he didn't, forced herself to go through with it. Stubborn pride on both their parts. And they were both so young, and this was so new to them. Six weeks the day after tomorrow.

She came bustling in, set down a little black valise in the middle of the room, and put on her gloves. Still waiting for him to make the first overtures for reconciliation. But he kept making the breach worse every time he opened his mouth, all because of what some fool had told him. "Sure you've got everything?" he said quietly.

She was so pretty even when she was angry. "I'm glad you're showing your true colors; I'd rather find out now than later."

Someone should have pushed their two heads together, probably. But there wasn't anyone around but just the two of them. "You're making a mountain out of a molehill. Well, pick a nice comfortable hotel while you're at it."

"I don't have to go to a hotel. I'm not a waif. I've got a perfectly good mother who'll receive me with open arms."

"Quite a trip in the middle of the night, isn't it?" And to make matters worse, he opened his wallet as if to give her the money for her fare.

That put the finishing touch to her exasperation. "I'll get up there without any help from you, Mr. Ed Bliss! And I don't want any of the things you ever gave me, either! Take your old silver-fox piece!" *Fluff.* "And take your old diamond ring!" *Plink.* "And take your old pin money!" *Scuff-scuff-slap.* "And you can take back that insurance policy you took out on me, too! Simon Legree! Ivan the Terrible!"

He turned the paper back to where the boxscores were. He only hoped that bachelor was right. "See you day after tomorrow, or whenever you get tired playing hide-and-seek," he said calmly.

"You'll never see me again as long as you live!" It rang in his ears for days afterwards.

She picked up the valise, the front door went *boom!* and he was single again.

The thing to do now was to pretend he didn't care, and then she'd never try anything like this again. Otherwise, his life would be made miserable. Every time they had the least little argument, she'd threaten to go back to her mother.

That first night he did all the things he'd always wanted to do, but they didn't stack up to so much after all. Took off his socks and walked around in his bare feet, let the ashes lie wherever they happened to drop off, drank six bottles of cold beer through their mouths and let them lie all over the room, and went to bed without bothering to shave.

He woke up about four in the morning, and it felt strange knowing she wasn't in the house with him, and he hoped she was all right wherever she was, and he finally forced himself to go back to sleep again. In the morning there wasn't anyone to wake him up. Her not being around didn't seem so strange then simply because he didn't have time to notice; he was exactly an hour and twenty-two minutes late for work.

But when he came back that night, it did seem strange, not finding anyone there waiting for him, the house dark and empty, and beer bottles rolling all around the living-room floor. Last night's meal, their last one together, was still strewn around on the table after twenty-four hours. He poked his finger at one of the biscuits, thought remorsefully, "I should have kept quiet. I could have pretended they were good, even if they weren't." But it was too late now; the damage had been done.

He had to eat out at a counter by himself, and it was very depressing. He picked up the phone twice that evening, at 10:30 and again at 11:22, on the point of phoning up to her mother's place and making up with her, or at least finding out how she was. But each time he sort of slapped his own hand, metaphorically speaking, in rebuke and hung up without putting the call through. "I'll hold out until tomorrow," he said to himself. "If I give in now, I'm at her mercy."

The second night was rocky. The bed was no good; they needed to be made up about once every twenty-four hours, he now found out for the first time. A cop poked him in the shoulder with his club at about three in the morning and growled, "What's your trouble, bud?"

"Nothing that's got anything to do with what's in your rule book," Bliss growled back at him. He picked himself up from the curb and went back inside his house again.

He would have phoned her as soon as he woke up in the morning, but he was late again—only twelve minutes be-hind, this time, though—and he couldn't do it from the office without his fellow draftsmen getting wise she had left him.

He finally did it when he came back that evening, the second time, after eating. This was exactly 8:17 p.m. Thursday, two nights after she'd gone.

He said, "I want to talk to Mrs. Belle Alden, in Denby, this state. I don't know her number. Find it for me and give it to me." He'd never met Smiles' mother, incidentally.

While he was waiting for the operator to ring back, he was still figuring how to get out of it; find out how she was without seeming to capitulate. Young pride! *Maybe I can talk the mother into not letting on I called to ask about her, so she won't know I'm weakening. Let it seem like she's the first one to thaw out.*

The phone rang and he picked it up fast, pride or no pride.

"Here's your party."

A woman's voice got on, and he said, "Hello, is this Mrs. Alden?"

The voice said it was.

"This is Ed, Smiles' husband."

"Oh, how is she?" she said animatedly.

He sat down at the phone. It took him a minute to get his breath back again. "Isn't she there?" he said finally.

The voice was surprised. "Here? No. Isn't she *there*?"

For a minute his stomach had felt all hollow. Now he was all right again. He was beginning to get it. Or thought he was. He winked at himself, with the wall in front of him for a reflector. So the mother was going to bat for her. They'd cooked up this little fib between them, to punish him. They were going to throw a little fright into him. He'd thought he was teaching her a lesson, and now she was going to turn the tables on him and teach him one. He was supposed to go rushing up there tearing at his hair and foaming at the mouth. "Where's Smiles? She's gone! I can't find her!" Then she'd step out from behind the door, crack her whip over his head, and threaten: "Are you going to behave? Are you ever going to do that again?" And from then on, she'd lead him around with a ring in his nose.

"You can't fool me, Mrs. Alden," he said self-assuredly. "I know she's there. I know she told you to say that."

Her voice wasn't panicky; it was still calm and self-possessed, but there was no mistaking the earnest ring to it. Either she was an awfully good actress, or this wasn't any act. "Now listen, Ed. You ought to know I wouldn't joke about a thing like that. As a matter of fact, I wrote her a long letter only yesterday afternoon. It ought to be in your mailbox by now. If she's not there with you, I'd make it my business to find out where she is, if I were you. And I wouldn't put it off, either!"

He still kept wondering: "Is she ribbing me or isn't she?" He drawled undecidedly, "Well, it's damned peculiar."

"I certainly agree with you," she said briskly. He just chewed the inner tube of his cheek.

"Well, will you let me know as soon as you find out where she is?" she concluded. "I don't want to worry, and naturally I won't be able to help doing so until I hear that she's all right."

He hung up, and first he was surer than ever that it wasn't true she wasn't there. For one thing, the mother hadn't seemed worried enough to make it convincing. He thought, "I'll be damned if I call back again, so you and she can have the laugh on me. She's up there with you right now."

But then he went outside and opened the mailbox, and there was a letter for Smiles with her mother's name on the envelope, and postmarked 6:30 the evening before.

He opened it and read it through. It was bona fide, all right; leisurely, chatty, nothing fake about it. One of those letters that are written over a period of days, a little at a time. There was no mistaking it; up to the time it had been mailed, she hadn't seen her daughter for months. And Smiles had left him the night before; if she'd gone up there at all, she would have been there long before then.

He didn't feel so chipper any more, after that. She

wouldn't have stayed away this long if she'd been here in town, where she could walk or take a cab back to the house. There was nothing to be that sore about. And she'd intended going up there. The reason he felt sure of that was this: With her, it wasn't a light decision, lightly taken and lightly discarded. She hadn't been living home with her mother when he married her. She'd been on her own down here for several years before then. They corresponded regularly, they were on good terms, but the mother's remarriage had made a difference. In other words, it wasn't a case of flying straight back to the nest the first time she'd lost a few feathers. It was not only a fairly lengthy trip up there, but they had not seen each other for several years. So if she'd said she was going up there, it was no fleeting impulse, but a rational, clear-cut decision, and she was the kind of girl who would carry it out once she had arrived at it.

He put his hat on, straightened his tie, left the house, and went downtown. There was only one way she could get anywhere near Denby, and that was by bus. It wasn't serviced by train.

Of the two main bus systems, one ran an express line that didn't stop anywhere near there; you had to go all the way to the Canadian border and then double back nearly half of the way by local, to get within hailing distance. The smaller line ran several a day, in each direction, up through there to the nearest large city beyond; they stopped there by request. It was obvious which of the two systems she'd taken.

That should have simplified matters greatly for him; he found out it didn't. He went down to the terminal and approached the ticket-seller.

"Were you on duty here Tuesday night?"

"Yeah, from six on. That's my shift every night."

"I'm trying to locate someone. Look. I know you're selling tickets all night long, but maybe you can remember her." He swallowed a lump in his throat. "She's young, only twenty, with blond hair. So pretty you'd look at her twice, if you ever saw her the first time; I know you would. Her eyes are sort of crinkly and smiling. Even when her mouth isn't smiling, her eyes are. She—she bought a ticket to Denby."

The man turned around and took a pack of tickets out of a pigeonhole and blew a layer of dust off them. "I haven't sold a ticket to Denby in over a month." They had a rubber band around them. All but the top one. That blew off with his breath.

That seemed to do something to his powers of memory. He ducked down out of sight, came up with it from the floor. "Wait a minute," he said, prodding his thumbnail between two of his teeth. "I don't remember anything much about any eyes or smile, but there was a young woman came up and priced the fare to Denby. I guess it was night before last, at that. Seeing this one ticket pulled loose out of the batch reminded me of it. I told her how much it was, and I snagged out a ticket—this loose one here. But then she couldn't make it; I dunno, she didn't have enough money on her or something. She looked at her wrist watch, and asked me how late the pawnshops stay open. I told her they were all closed by then. Then she shoveled all the money she could round up across the counter at me and asked me how far that would take her. So I counted and told her, and she told me to give her a ticket to that far."

Bliss was hanging onto his words, hands gripping the counter until his knuckles showed white. "Yes, but where to?"

The ticket-seller's eyelids drooped deprecatingly. "That's the trouble," he said, easing the back of his collar. "I can't remember that part of it. I can't even remember how much the amount came to, now, any more. If I could, I could get the destination by elimination."

"If I only knew how much she had in her handbag when she left the house," Bliss thought desolately, "we could work it out together, him and me." He prodded: "Three dollars? Four? Five?"

The ticket vendor shook his head baffledly. "No use, it won't come back. I'm juggling so many figures all night long, every night in the week—"

Bliss slumped lower before the sill. "But don't you keep a record of what places you sell tickets to?"

"No, just the total take for the night, without breaking it down."

He was as bad off as before. "Then you can't tell me for sure whether she did get on the bus that night or not?"

Meanwhile an impatient line had formed behind Bliss, and the ticket-seller was getting fidgety.

"No. The driver might remember her. Look at it this way: she only stood in front of me for a minute or two at the most. If she got on the bus at all, she sat in back of him for anywhere from an hour to four hours. Remember, I'm not even guaranteeing that the party I just told you about is the same one you mean. It's just a vague incident to me."

"Would the same one that made Tuesday night's run be back by now?"

"Sure, he's going out tonight again." The ticket man looked at a chart. "Go over there and ask for No. 27. Next!"

No. 27 put down his coffee mug, swiveled around on the counter stool, and looked at his questioner.

"Yare, I made Tuesday night's upstate run."

"Did you take a pretty blond girl, dressed in a gray jacket and skirt, as far as Denby?"

No. 27 stopped looking at him. His face stayed on in the same direction, but he was looking at other things. "Nawr, I didn't."

"Well, was she on the bus at all?"

No. 27's eyes remained at a tangent from the man he was answering. "Nawr, she wasn't."

"What're you acting so evasive about? I can tell you're hiding something, just by looking at you."

"I said, 'Nawr, I didn't.' "

"Listen. I'm her husband. I've got to know. Here, take this, only tell me, will you? I've got to know. It's an awful feeling!"

The driver took a hitch in his belt. "I get good wages. A

ten-dollar bill wouldn't make me say I sawr someone when I
didn't. No, nor a twenty, nor a century either. That's an old
one. It would only make me lose my rating with the company." He swung around on his stool, took up his coffee
mug again. "I only sawr the road," he said truculently. "I
ain't supposed to see who's riding in back of me."

"But you can't help seeing who gets off each time you
stop."

This time No. 27 wouldn't answer at all. The interview
was over, as far as he was concerned. He flung down a
nickel, defiantly jerked down the visor of his cap, and swag-
gered off.

Bliss slouched forlornly out of the terminal, worse off
than before. The issue was all blurred now. The ticket-seller
vaguely thought some girl or other had haphazardly bought
a ticket for as much money as she had on her person that
night, but without guaranteeing that she fitted his description of Smiles at all. The driver, on the other hand, definitely
denied anyone like her had ridden with him, as far as Denby
or anywhere else. What was he to think? Had she left, or
hadn't she left?

Whether she had or not, it was obvious that she had
never arrived. He had the testimony of her own mother, and
that letter from her from upstate, to vouch for that. And
who was better to be believed than her own mother?

Had she stayed here in the city then? But she hadn't done
that, either. He knew Smiles so well. Even if she had gone
to the length of staying overnight at a hotel that first night,
Tuesday, she would have been back home with him by
Wednesday morning at the very latest. Her peevishness
would have evaporated long before then. Another thing, she
wouldn't have had enough money to stay for any longer
than just one night at even a moderately priced hotel. She'd
flung down the greater part of her household expense
money on the floor that night before walking out.

"All I can do," he thought apprehensively, "is make a
round of the hotels and find out if anyone like her was at

any of them Tuesday night, even if she's not there now."

He didn't check every last hotel in town, but he checked all the ones she would have gone to, if she'd gone to one at all. She wouldn't have been sappy enough to go to some rundown lodging-house near the freight yards or long-shoremen's hostelry down by the piers. That narrowed the field somewhat.

He checked on her triply: by name first, on the hotel registers for Tuesday night; then by her description, given to the desk clerks; and lastly by any and all entries in the registers, no matter what name was given. He knew her handwriting, even if she'd registered under an assumed name.

He drew a complete blank. No one who looked like her had come to any of the hotels—Tuesday night, or at any time since. No one giving her name. No one giving another name, who wrote like her. What was left? Where else could she have gone? Friends? She didn't have any. Not close ones, not friends she knew well enough to walk in on unannounced and stay overnight with.

Where was she? She wasn't in the city. She wasn't in the country, up at Denby. She seemed to have vanished completely from the face of the earth.

It was past two in the morning by the time he'd finished checking the hotels. It was too late to get a bus any more that night, or he would have gone up to Denby then and there himself. He turned up his coat collar against the night mist and started disconsolately homeward. On the way he tried to buck himself up by saying: "Nothing's happened to her. She's just hiding out somewhere, trying to throw a scare into me. She'll show up, she's bound to." It wouldn't work, much. It was two whole days and three nights now. Marriage is learning to know another person, learning to know by heart what he or she'd do in such-and-such a situation. They'd only been married six weeks, but, after all, they'd been going together nearly a year before that; he knew her pretty well by now.

She wasn't vindictive. She didn't nurse grievances, even

imaginary ones. There were only two possible things she would have done. She would have either gotten on that bus red-hot, been cooled off long before she got off it again, but stayed up there a couple of days as long as she was once there. Or if she hadn't taken the bus, she would have been back by twelve at the latest right that same night, with an injured air and a remark like: "You ought to be ashamed of yourself letting your wife walk the streets like a vagrant!" or something to that effect. She hadn't, so she must have gone up there. Then he thought of the letter from her mother, and he felt good and scared.

The phone was ringing when he got back. He could hear it even before he got the front door open. He nearly broke the door down in his hurry to get at it. For a minute he thought—

But it was only Mrs. Alden. She said, "I've been trying to get you ever since ten o'clock. I didn't hear from you, and I've been getting more and more worried." His heart went down under his shoelaces. "Did you locate her? Is it all right?"

"I can't find her," he said, so low he had to say it over again so she could catch it.

She'd been talking fast until now. Now she didn't say anything at all for a couple of minutes; there was just an empty hum on the wire. Something came between them. They'd never seen each other face to face, but he could sense a change in her voice, a different sound to it the next time he heard it. It was as though she were drawing away from him. Not moving from where she stood, of course, but rather withdrawing her confidence. The beginnings of suspicion were lurking in it somewhere or other.

"Don't you think it's high time you got in touch with the police?" he heard her say. And then, so low that he could hardly get it: "If you don't, I will." *Click*, and she was gone.

He didn't take it the way he, perhaps, should have.

As he hung up, he thought, "Yes, she's right, I'll have to. Nothing else left to be done now. It's two full days now; no use kidding myself any more."

He put on his hat and coat again, left the house once more. It was about three in the morning by this time. He hated to go to them. It seemed like writing *finis* to it. It seemed to make it so final, tragic, in a way. As though, once he notified them, all hope of her returning to him unharmed, of her own accord, was over. As though it stopped being just a little private, domestic matter any more and became a police matter, out of his own hands. Ridiculous, he knew, but that was the way he felt about it. But it had to be done. Just sitting worrying about her wasn't going to bring her back.

He went in between two green door lamps and spoke to a desk sergeant. "I want to report my wife missing." They sent a man out, a detective, to talk to him. Then he had to go down to the city morgue, to see if she was among the unidentified dead there, and that was the worst experience he'd had yet. It wasn't the sight of the still faces one by one; it was the dread, each time, that the next one would be hers. Half under his breath, each time he shook his head and looked at someone who had once been loved, he added, "No, thank God." She wasn't there.

Although he hadn't found her, all he could give when he left the place of the dead was a sigh of unutterable relief. She wasn't among the found dead; that was all this respite marked. But he knew, although he tried to shut the grisly thought out, that there are many dead who are not found. Sometimes not right away, sometimes never.

They took him around to the hospitals then, to certain wards, and though this wasn't quite so bad as the other place, it wasn't much better either. He looked for her among amnesia victims, would-be suicides who had not yet recovered consciousness, persons with all the skin burned off their faces, mercifully swathed in gauze bandaging and tea leaves. They even made him look in the alcoholic wards, though he protested strenuously that she wouldn't be there, and in the psychopathic wards.

The sigh of relief he gave when this tour was over was only less heartfelt than after leaving the morgue. She wasn't dead. She wasn't maimed or injured or out of her mind in any way. And still she wasn't to be found.

Then they turned it over to Missing Persons, had her description broadcast, and told him there wasn't anything he could do for the present but go home.

He didn't even try to sleep when he got back the second time. Just sat there waiting—for the call that didn't come and that he somehow knew wouldn't come, not if he waited for a week or a month.

It was starting to get light by that time. The third day since she'd been swallowed up bodily was dawning. She wasn't in the city, alive or dead, he was convinced. Why sit there waiting for them to locate her when he was sure she wasn't here? He'd done all he could at this end. He hadn't done anything yet at the other end. The thing was too serious now; it wasn't enough just to take the word of a *voice* over a telephone wire that she wasn't up there. Not even if the voice was that of her own mother, who was to be trusted if anyone was, who thought as much of her as he did. He decided he'd go up there himself. Anything was better than just sitting here waiting helplessly.

He couldn't take the early-morning bus, the way he wanted to. Those building plans he was finishing up had to be turned in today; there was an important contractor waiting for them. He stood there poring over the blueprints, more dead than alive between worry and lack of sleep, and when they were finally finished, turned in, and O.K.'d, he went straight from the office to the terminal and took the bus that should get in there about dark.

Denby wasn't even an incorporated village, he found when the bus finally got there, an hour late. It was just a place where a turnpike crossed another road, with houses spaced at lengthy intervals along the four arms of the intersection. Some of them a quarter of a mile apart, few of them in full view of one another due to intervening trees, bends in the roads, rises and dips of the ground. A filling-station was the nearest thing to the crossroads, in one direction. Up in the other was a store, with living-quarters over it. It was the most dispersed community he had ever seen.

He chose the store at random, stopped in there, and asked, "Which way to the Alden house?"

The storekeeper seemed to be one of those people who wear glasses for the express purpose of staring over instead of through them. Or maybe they'd slipped down on the bridge of his nose. "Take that other fork, to your right," he instructed. "Just keep going till you think there ain't going to be no more houses, and you're sure I steered you wrong. Keep on going anyway. When you least expect it, one last house'll show up, round the turn. That's them. Can't miss it. You'll know it by the low brick barrier wall runs along in front of it. He put that up lately, just to keep in practice, I reckon."

Bliss wondered what he meant by that, if anything, but didn't bother asking. The storekeeper was evidently one of these loquacious souls who would have rambled on forever given the slightest encouragement, and Bliss was tired and anxious to reach his destination. He thanked him and left.

The walk out was no picayune city block or two; it was a good stiff hike. The road stretched before him like a white tape under the velvety night sky, dark-blue rather than black, and stars twinkled down through the openings between the roadside-tree branches. He could hear countryside night noises around him, crickets or something, and once a dog barked way off in the distance—it sounded like miles away. It was lonely, but not particularly frightening. Nature rarely is; it is man that is menacing.

Just the same, if she had come up here—and of course she hadn't—it wouldn't have been particularly prudent for a young girl alone like her to walk this distance at that hour of the night. She probably would have phoned out to them to come in and meet her at the crossroads, from either the store or that filling-station. And yet if both had been closed up by then—her bus wouldn't have passed through here until one or two in the morning—she would have had to walk it alone. But she hadn't come up so why conjure up additional dangers?

Thinking which, he came around the slow turn in the road and a low, elbow-height boundary wall sprang up beside him and ran down the road past a pleasant, white-painted two-story house, with dark gables, presumably green. They seemed to keep it in good condition. As for the wall itself, he got what the storekeeper's remark had intended to convey when he saw it. It looked very much as though Alden had put it up simply to kill time, give himself something to do, add a fancy touch to his property. For it seemed to serve no useful purpose. It was not nearly high enough to shut off the view, so it had not been built for privacy. It only ran along the front of the parcel, did not extend around the sides or to the back, so it was not even effective as a barrier against poultry or cattle, or useful as a boundary mark. It seemed to be purely decorative. As such, it was a neat, workmanlike job; you could tell Alden had been a mason before his marriage. It was brick, smoothly, painstakingly plastered over.

There was no gate in it, just a gap, with an ornamental willow wicket arched high over it. He turned in through there. They were up yet, though perhaps already on the point of retiring. One of the upper-floor windows held a light, but with a blind discreetly drawn down over it.

He rang the bell, then stepped back from the door and looked up, expecting to be interrogated first from the window, particularly at this hour. Nothing of the kind happened; they evidently possessed the trustfulness that goes with a clear conscious. He could hear steps start down the inside stairs. A woman's steps, at that, and a voice that carried out to where he was with surprising clarity said, "Must be somebody lost their way, I guess."

A hospitable little lantern up over the door went on from the inside, and a moment later he was looking at a pleasant-faced, middle-aged woman with soft gray eyes. Her face was long and thin, but without the hatchet-sharp features that are so often an accompaniment of that contour of face. Her hair was a graying blond, but soft and wavy, not scraggly. Knowing who she was, he almost thought he could detect a little bit of Smiles in her face: the shape of the brows and the curve of the mouth, but that might have been just auto-suggestion.

"Hm-m-m?" she said serenely.

"I'm Ed, Mrs. Alden."

She blinked twice, as though she didn't get it for a minute. Or maybe wasn't expecting it.

"Smiles' husband," he said, a trifle irritatedly. You're supposed to know your own in-laws. It wasn't their fault, of course, that they didn't. It wasn't his, either. He and Smiles had been meaning to come up here on a visit as soon as they could, but they'd been so busy getting their own home together, and six weeks is such a short time. Her mother had been getting over a prolonged illness at the time of their wedding, hadn't been strong enough for the trip down and back.

Both her hands came out toward his now, after that momentary blankness. "Oh, come in, Ed," she said heartily. "I've been looking forward to meeting you, but I *wish* it had been under other circumstances." She glanced past his shoulder. "She's not with you, I see. No word yet, Ed?" she went on worriedly.

He looked down and shook his head glumly.

She held her hand to her mouth in involuntary dismay, then quickly recovered her self-control, as though not wishing to add to his distress. "Don't know what to think," she murmured half audibly. "It's not like her to do a thing like that. Have you been to the police yet, Ed?"

"I reported it to them before daylight this morning. Had to go around to the different hospitals and places." He blew out his breath at the recollection. "*Huff,* it was ghastly."

"Don't let's give up yet, Ed. You know the old saying,

'No news is good news.' " Then: "Don't let me keep you standing out here. Joe's upstairs; I'll call him down."

As he followed her inside, his whole first impression of Smiles' mother was that she was as nice, wholesome, and inartificial a woman as you could find anywhere. And first impressions are always half the battle.

She led him along a neat, hardwood-floored hall, varnished to the brightness of a mirror. An equally spotless white staircase rose at the back of it to the floor above.

"Let me take your hat," she said thoughtfully, and hung it on a peg. "You look peaked, Ed; I can tell you're taking it hard. That trip up is strenuous, too. It's awful; you know you read about things like this in the papers nearly every day, but it's only when it hits home you realize—"

Talking disconnectedly like that, she had reached the entrance to the living-room. She thrust her hand around to the inside of the door frame and snapped on the lights. He was standing directly in the center of the opening as she did so. There was something a little unexpected about the way they went on, but he couldn't figure what it was; it must have been just a subconscious impression on his part. Maybe they were a little brighter than he'd expected, and after coming in out of the dark— The room looked as though it had been painted fairly recently, and he supposed that was what it was: the walls and woodwork gave it back with unexpected dazzle. It was too small a detail even to waste time on. Or is any detail ever too small?

She had left him for a moment to go as far as the foot of the stairs. "Joe, Smiles' husband is here," he heard her call.

A deep rumbling voice answered, "She with him?"

She tactfully didn't answer that, no doubt to spare Bliss's feelings; she seemed to be such a considerate woman. "Come down, dear," was all she said.

He was a thick, heavy-set man, with a bull neck and a little circular fringe of russet-blond hair around his head, the crown of it bald. He was going to be the blunt, aggressive type, Bliss could see. With eyes too small to match it. Eyes that said, "Try and get past us."

"So you're Bliss." He reached out and shook hands with him. It was a hard shake, but not particularly friendly. His hands were calloused to the lumpiness of alligator hide. "Well, you're taking it pretty calmly, it seems to me."

Bliss looked at him. "How do you figure that?"

"Joe!" the mother had remonstrated, but so low neither of them paid any attention.

"Coming up here like this. Don't you think it's your business to stick close down there, where you could do some good?"

Mrs. Alden laid a comforting hand on Bliss's arm. "Don't, Joe. You can tell how the boy feels by looking at him. I'm Smiles' mother and I know how it is; if she said she was coming up here, why, naturally—"

"I know you're Teresa's mother," he said emphatically, as if to shut her up.

A moment of awkward silence hung suspended in the air above their three heads. Bliss had a funny "lost" feeling for a minute, as though something had eluded him just then, something had been a little askew. It was like when there's a word you are trying desperately to remember; it's on the tip of your tongue, but you can't bring it out. It was such a small thing, though—

"I'll get you something to eat, Ed," she said, and as she turned to go out of the room, Bliss couldn't help overhearing her say to her husband in a stage whisper: "Talk to him. Find out what really happened."

Alden had about as much finesse as a trained elephant doing the gavotte among ninepins. He cleared his throat judicially. "D'ja do something you shouldn't? That how it come about?"

"What do you mean?"

"Wull, *we* have no way of knowing what kind of a disposition you've got. Have you got a pretty bad temper, are you a little too quick with the flat of your hand?"

Bliss looked at him incredulously. Then he got it. "That's

hardly a charge I expected to have to defend myself on. But if it's required of me—I happen to worship the ground my wife walks on. I'd sooner have my right arm wither away than—"

"No offense," said Alden lamely. "It's been known to happen before, that's all."

"Not in my house," Bliss said, and gave him a steely look.

Smiles' mother came in again at this point, with something on a tray. Bliss didn't even bother looking up to see what it was. He waved it aside, sat there with his arms dangling out over his knees, his head bent way over, looking straight down through them.

The room was a vague irritant. He kept getting it all the time, at least every time he raised his head and looked around, but he couldn't figure what was doing it. There was only one thing he was sure of: it wasn't the people in it. So that left it up to the room. Smiles' mother was the soothing, soft-moving type that it was pleasant to have around you. And even the husband, in spite of his brusqueness, was the stolid emotionless sort that didn't get on your nerves.

What was it, then? Was the room furnished in bad taste? It wasn't; it was comfortable and homey-looking. And even if it hadn't been, that wouldn't have done it. He was no interior decorator, allergic to anything like that. Was it the glare from the recent paint job? No, not that, either; now that he looked, there wasn't any glare. It wasn't even glossy paint; it was the dull kind without highlights. That had just been an optical illusion when the lights first went on.

He shook his head a little to get rid of it, and thought, "What's annoying me in here?" And he couldn't tell.

He was holding a lighted cigarette between his dangling fingers, and the ash was slowly accumulating.

"Pass him an ash tray, Joe," she said in a watery voice. She was starting to cry, without any fuss, unnoticeably, but she still had time to think of their guest's comfort. Some women are like that.

He looked and a whole cylinder of ash had fallen to the

rug. It looked like a good rug, too. "I'm sorry," he said, and rubbed it out with his shoe. Even the rug bothered him in some way.

Pattern too loud? No, it was quiet, dark-colored, and in good taste. He couldn't find a thing the matter with it. But it kept troubling him just the same.

Something went *clang*. It wasn't in the same room with them; some other part of the house, faint and muffled, like a defective pipe joint settling or swelling.

She said, "Joe, when are you going to have the plumber in to fix that water pipe? It's sprung out of line again. You'll wait until we have a good-sized leak on our hands."

"Yeah, that's right," he said. It sounded more like an original discovery than a recollection of something overlooked. Bliss couldn't have told why, it just did. More of his occultism, he supposed.

"I'll have to get a fresh handkerchief," she said apologetically, got up and passed between them, the one she had been using until now rolled into a tight little ball at her upper lip.

"Take it easy," Alden said consolingly.

His eyes went to Bliss, then back to her again, as if to say: "Do you see that she's crying, as well as I do?" So Bliss glanced at her profile as she went by, and she was. She ought to have been; she was the girl's mother.

When she came in again with the fresh handkerchief she'd gone to get, he got to his feet.

"This isn't bringing her back. I'd better get down to the city again. They might have word for me by now."

Alden said, "Can I talk to you alone a minute, Bliss, before you go?"

The three of them had moved out into the hall. Mrs. Alden went up the stairs slowly. The higher up she got the louder her sobs became. Finally, a long wail burst out, and the closing of a door cut it in half. A minute later bedsprings protested, as if someone had dropped on them full length.

"D'you hear that?" Alden said to him. Another of those

never-ending nuances hit Bliss; he'd said it as if he were proud of it.

Bliss was standing in the doorway, looking back into the room. He felt as if he were glad to get out of it. And he still couldn't understand why, any more than any of the rest of it.

"What was it you wanted to say to me on the side?"

Blunt as ever, Alden asked, "Have you told us everything, or have you left out part of it? Just what went on between you and Teresa anyway?"

"One of those tiffs."

Alden's small eyes got even smaller; they almost creased out in his face. "It must have been *some* tiff, for her to walk out on you with her grip in her hand. She wasn't the kind—"

"How did you know she took her grip with her? I didn't tell you that."

"You didn't have to. She was coming up here, wasn't she? They always take their grips when they walk out on you."

There wasn't pause enough between their two sentences to stick a bent comma. One just seemed to flow out of the other, only with a change of speakers. Alden's voice had gone up a little with the strain of the added pace he'd put into it, that was all. He'd spoken it a little faster than his usual cadence. Small things. Damn those small things to hell, torturing him like gnats, like gnats that you can't put your finger on!

Right under Bliss's eyes, a bead of sweat was forming between two of the reddish tufts of hair at the edge of Alden's hairline. He could see it oozing out of the pore. What was that from? Just from discussing what time his bus would get him back to the city, as they were doing now? No, it must have been from saying that sentence too fast a while ago—the one about the grip. The effects were only coming out now.

"Well," Bliss said, "I'd better get a move on, to catch the bus back."

Her door, upstairs, had opened again. It might have been just coincidental, but it was timed almost as though she'd been listening.

"Joe," she called down the stairwell. "Don't let Ed start back down again right tonight. Two trips in one day is too much; he'll be a wreck. Why not have him stay over with us tonight, and take the early morning one instead?"

Bliss was standing right down there next to him. She could have spoken to him directly just as easily. Why did she have to relay it through her husband?

"Yeah," Alden said up to her, "that's just what I was thinking myself." But it was as though he'd said: "I get you."

Bliss had a funny feeling they'd been saying something to one another right in front of his face without his knowing what it was.

"No," he said dolefully, "I'm worried about her. The sooner I get down there and get to the bottom of it—"

He went on out the door, and Alden came after him.

"I'll walk you down to the bus stop," he offered.

"Not necessary," Bliss told him curtly. After all, twice now this other man had tried to suggest he'd abused or maltreated his wife; he couldn't help resenting it. "I can find my way back without any trouble. You're probably tired and want to turn in."

"Just as you say," Alden acquiesced.

They didn't shake hands at parting. Bliss couldn't help noticing that the other man didn't even reach out and offer to. For his part, that suited him just as well.

After he'd already taken a few steps down the road, Alden called out after him, "Let us know the minute you get good news; I don't want my wife to worry any more than she has to. She's taking it hard."

Bliss noticed he didn't include himself in that. He didn't hold that against him, though; after all, there was no blood relationship there.

Alden turned as if to go back inside the house again, but when Bliss happened to glance back several minutes later, just before taking the turn in the road that cut the house off from sight, he could still detect a narrow up-and-down band of light escaping from the doorway, with a break in it at one point as though a protruding profile were obscuring it.

"Wants to make sure I'm really on my way to take that bus," he said to himself knowingly. But suspicion is a two-edged sword that turns against the wielder as readily as the one it is wielded against. He only detected the edge that was turned toward him, and even that but vaguely.

He reached the crossroads and took up his position. He still had about five minutes to wait, but he'd hardly arrived when two yellow peas of light, swelling until they became great hazy balloons, came down the turnpike toward him. He thought it was the bus at first, ahead of its own schedule, but it turned out to be a coupe with a Quebec license. It slowed long enough for the occupant to lean out and ask:

"Am I on the right road for the city?"

"Yeah, keep going straight, you can't miss," Bliss said dully. Then suddenly, on an impulse he was unable to account for afterward, he raised his voice and called out after him, "Hey! I don't suppose you'd care to give me a lift in with you?"

"Why not?" the Canuck said amiably, and slowed long enough for Bliss to catch up to him.

Bliss opened the door and sidled in. He still didn't know what had made him change his mind like this, unless perhaps it was the vague thought that he might make better time in with a private car like this than he would have with the bus.

The driver said something about being glad to have someone to talk to on the way down, and Bliss explained briefly that he'd been waiting for the bus, but beyond those few introductory remarks, they did not talk much. Bliss wanted to think. He wanted to analyze his impression of the visit he had just concluded.

It was pretty hopeless to do much involved thinking with a stranger at his elbow, liable to interrupt his train of thought every once in a while with some unimportant remark that had to be answered for courtesy's sake, so the most he could do was marshal his impressions, sort of document them for future reference when he was actually alone:

1. The lights seemed to go on in an unexpected way, when she first pressed the switch.

2. The room bothered him. It hadn't been the kind of room you feel at ease in. It hadn't been *restful*.

3. There had been some sort of faulty vocal coordination when she said, "I'm Smiles' mother," and he said, "I know you're Teresa's mother."

4. There had also been nuances in the following places: When Alden's eyes sought his, as if to assure himself that he, Bliss, saw that she was crying almost unnoticeably there in the room with them. When she ran whimpering up the stairs and threw herself on the bed, and he said, "Hear that?" And lastly when she called down and addressed her overnight invitation to Alden, instead of Bliss himself, as though there were some intangible kernel in it to be extracted first before he passed on the dry husk of the words themselves to Bliss.

At this point, before he got any further, there was a thud, a long-drawn-out reptilian hiss, and a tire went out. They staggered to a stop at the side of the road.

"Looks like I've brought you tough luck," Bliss remarked.

"No," his host assured him, "that thing's been on its ninth life for weeks; I'm only surprised it lasted this long. I had it patched before I left Three Rivers this morning, thought maybe I could make the city on it, but it looks like no soap. Well, I have a spare, and now I *am* glad I hitched you on; four hands are better than two."

The stretch of roadway where it had happened was a particularly bad one, Bliss couldn't help noticing as he slung off his coat and jumped down to lend a hand; it was crying for attention, needled with small jagged rock fragments, either improperly crushed in the first place or else loosened from their bed by some recent rain. He supposed it hadn't been blocked off because there was no other branch road in the immediate vicinity that could take its place as a detour.

They'd hardly gotten the jack out when the bus overtook and passed them, wiping out his gain of time at a stroke. And then, a considerable time later, after they'd already finished the job and wiped their hands clean, some other anonymous car went steaming by, this time at a rate of speed that made the bus seem to have been standing still in its tracks. The Canadian was the only one in sight by the stalled car as its comet-like headlights flicked by. Bliss happened to be farther in off the road just then. He turned his head and looked after it, however, at the tornado-like rush of air that followed in its wake, and got a glimpse of it just before it hurtled from sight.

"That fellow's *asking* for a flat," the Canadian said, "passing over a stretch of fill like this at such a clip."

"He didn't have a spare on him, either," Bliss commented.

"Looked like he was trying to beat that bus in." Just an idle phrase, for purposes of comparison. It took on new meaning later, though, when Bliss remembered it.

They climbed in and started off again. The rest of the ride passed uneventfully. Bliss spelled his companion at the wheel, the last hour in, and let him take a little doze. He'd been on the road steadily since early that morning, he'd told Bliss.

Bliss woke him up and gave the car back to him when they reached the city limits. The Canadian was heading for a certain hotel all the way downtown, so Bliss wouldn't let him deviate from his course to take him over to his place; he got out instead at the nearest parallel point to it they touched, thanked him, and started over on foot.

He had a good stiff walk ahead of him, but he didn't mind that—he'd been sitting cramped up for so long. He still wanted to think things over as badly as ever, too, and he'd found out by experience that solitary walking helped him to think better.

It didn't in this case, though. He was either too tired from the events of the past few days, or else the materials he had were too formless, indefinite, to get a good grip on. He kept asking himself, "What was wrong up there? Why am I dissatisfied?" And he couldn't answer for the life of him. "Was anything wrong," he was finally reduced to wondering, "or was it wholly imaginary on my part?" It was like a wrestling bout with shadows.

The night around him was dark-blue velvet, and as he drew near his own isolated semi-suburban neighborhood, the silence was at least equal to that up at Denby. There wasn't a soul stirring, not even a milkman. He trudged onward under a leafy tunnel of sidewalk trees that all but made him invisible.

Leaving the coupe where he had, and coming over in a straight line this way, brought him up to his house from behind, on the street in back of it instead of the one running directly before it, which was an approach he never took at other times, such as when coming home from downtown. Behind it there was nothing but vacant plots, so it was a shortcut to cross diagonally behind the house next door and go through from the back instead of going all the way around the corner on the outside. He did that now, without thinking of anything except to save a few extra steps.

As he came out from behind the house next door, treading soundless on the well-kept backyard grass, he saw a momentary flash through one of his own windows that could only have been a pocket torch. He stopped dead in his tracks. *Burglars* was the first thought that came to him.

He advanced a wary step or two. The flash came again, but from another window this time, nearer the front. They were evidently on their way out, using it only intermittently to help find their way. He'd be able to head them off at the front door, as they stole forth.

There was a partition hedge between the two houses, running from front to back. He scurried along that, on his neighbor's side of it, keeping head and shoulders down, until he was on a line with his own front door. He crouched there, peering through.

They had left a lookout standing just outside his door. He could see the motionless figure. And then, as his fingers were about to part the hedge, to aid him in crashing through, the still form shifted a little, and the uncertain light struck a glint from a little wedge on its chest. At the same instant Bliss caught the outline of a visor above the profile. A cop!

One hand behind him, Bliss ebbed back again on his heels, thrown completely off balance by the unexpected revelation.

His own front door opened just then and two men came out, one behind the other. Without visors and without metallic gleams on their chests. But the cop turned and flipped up his nightstick toward them in semi-salute; so, whatever they were, they weren't burglars, although one was unmistakably carrying something out of the house with him.

They carefully closed the front door behind them, even tried it a second time to make sure it was securely fastened. A snatch of guarded conversation drifted toward him as they made their way down the short front walk to the sidewalk. The uniformed man took no part in it, only the two who had been inside.

"He's hot, all right," Bliss heard one say.

"Sure, he's hot, and he already knows it. You notice he wasn't on that bus when it got in. I'll beat it down and get the Teletype busy. You put a case on this place. Still, he might try to sneak back in again later."

Bliss had been crouched there on his heels. He went forward and down now on the flats of his hands, as stunned as though he'd gotten a rabbit punch at the back of the neck.

Motionless there, almost dazed, he kept shaking his head slightly, as though to clear it. They were after *him*; they thought he'd— Not only that, but they'd been tipped off what bus he was supposed to show up on. That could mean only one person, Joe Alden.

He wasn't surprised. He could even understand his doing a thing like that; it must seem suspicious to them up there the way she'd disappeared, and Bliss's own complete lack of any plausible explanation for it. He'd probably have felt the same way about it himself, if he'd been in their place. But he did resent the sneaky way Alden had gone about it, waiting until he was gone and then denouncing him the minute his back was turned. Why hadn't he tried to have him held by the locals while he was right up there with them? He supposed, now, that was the esoteric meaning in her invitation to him to stay over; so Alden could go out and bring in the cops while he was asleep under their roof. It hadn't worked because he'd insisted on leaving.

Meanwhile, he continued watching these men before him who had now, through no fault of his own, become his deadly enemies. They separated. One of them, with the uniformed cop trailing along with him, started down the street away from the house. The other drifted diagonally across to the opposite side. The gloom of an overshadowing tree over there swallowed him, and he failed to show up again on the other side of it, where there was a little more light.

There was hardly any noise about the whole thing, hardly so much as a footfall. They were like shadows moving in a dream world. A car engine began droning stealthily, slurred away, from a short distance farther down the street, marking the point of departure of two out of the three. A drop of sweat, as cold as mercury, toiled sluggishly down the nape of Bliss's neck, blotted itself into his collar.

He stayed there where he was, on all fours behind the hedge, a few minutes longer. The only thing to do was go out and try to clear himself. The only thing not to do was turn around and slink off—though the way lay open behind him. But at the same time he had a chill premonition that it wasn't going to be so easy to clear himself; that once they got their hands on him—

"But I've got to," he kept telling himself over and over.

"They've got to help me, not go after me. They can't say I—
did anything like that to Smiles! Maybe I can hit one of them
that's fair minded, will listen to me."

Meanwhile he had remained in the crouched position of a
track runner waiting for the signal to start. He picked himself up slowly and straightened to his full height behind the
hedge. That took courage, alone, without moving a step farther. "Well, here goes," he muttered, tightened his belt, and
stuck a cigarette in his mouth. It was a crawly sort of feeling.
He knew, nine chances to one, his freedom of movement
was over the minute he stepped out from behind this hedge
and went over toward that inky tree shadow across the
street that was just a little too lumpy in the middle. He
didn't give a rap about freedom of movement in itself, but
his whole purpose, his one aim from now on, was to look
for and find Smiles. He was afraid losing it would hamper
him in that. She was his wife; he wanted to look for her
himself. He didn't want other guys to do it for him whether
they were professionals or not.

He lighted the cigarette when halfway across the street,
but the tree shadow didn't move. The detective evidently
didn't know him by sight yet, was on the lookout for someone coming from the other direction on his way to the
house.

Bliss stopped right in front of him and said, "Are you
looking for me? I'm Ed Bliss and I live over there."

The shadow up and down the tree trunk detached itself,
became a man. "How'd you know anyone was looking for
you?" It was a challenge, as though that were already an ad-
mission of guilt in itself.

Bliss said, "Come inside, will you? I want to talk to you."

They crossed over once more. Bliss unlocked the door
for him, with his own key this time, and put on the lights.
They went into the living-room. It was already getting dusty
from not being cleaned in several days.

He looked Bliss over good. Bliss looked him over just as
good. He wanted a man in this, not a detective.

The detective spoke first, repeated what he'd asked him outside on the street. "How'd you know we'd be looking for you when that bus got in?"

"I didn't. I just happened to take a lift down instead."

"What's become of your wife, Bliss?"

"I don't know."

"We think you do."

"I wish you were right. But not in the way you mean."

"Never mind what you wish. You know another good word for that? Remorse."

The blood in Bliss's face thinned a little. "Before you put me in the soup, just let me talk here quietly with you a few minutes. That's all I ask."

"When she walked out of here Tuesday night, what was she wearing?"

Bliss hesitated a minute. Not because he didn't know— he'd already described her outfit to them when he reported her missing—but because he could sense a deeper import lurking behind the question.

The detective took the hesitancy for an attempt at evasion, went on: "Now, every man knows his wife's clothes by heart. You paid for every last one of them; you know just what she owned. Just tell me what she had on."

There was danger in it somewhere. "She had on a gray suit—jacket and skirt, you know. Then a pink silk shirtwaist. She threw her fur piece back at me, so that's about all she went out in. A hat, of course. One of those crazy hats."

"Baggage?"

"A black valise with tan binding. Oh, about the size of a typewriter case."

"Sure of that?"

"Sure of that."

The detective gave a kind of soundless whistle through his teeth.

"Whe-ew!" he said, and he looked at Bliss almost as if he felt sorry for him. "You've sure made it tough for yourself this time! I didn't have to ask you that, because we know just as well as you what she had on."

"How?"

"Because we found every last one of those articles you just mentioned in the furnace downstairs in this very house, less than twenty minutes ago. My partner's gone down to headquarters with them. And a guy don't do that to his wife's clothes unless he's done something to his wife, too. What've you done with her, Bliss?"

The other man wasn't even in the room with him any more, so far as Bliss was concerned. A curtain of foggy horror had dropped down all around him. "My God!" he whispered hoarsely. "Something's happened to her, somebody's done something to her!" And he jumped up and ran out of the room so unexpectedly, so swiftly, that if his purpose had been to escape, he almost could have eluded the other man. Instead, he made for the cellar door and ran down the basement steps. The detective had shot to his feet after him, was at his heels by the time he got down to the bottom. Bliss turned on the light and looked at the furnace grate, yawning emptily open—as though that could tell him anything more.

He turned despairingly to the detective. "Was there any blood on them?"

"Should there have been?"

"Don't! Have a heart," Bliss begged in a choked voice, and shaded his eyes. "Who put them in there? Why'd they bring them back here? How'd they get in while I was out?"

"Quit that," the headquarters man said dryly. "Suppose we get started. Our guys'll be looking all over for you, and it'll save them a lot of trouble."

Every few steps on the way back up those basement stairs, Bliss would stop, as though he'd run down and needed winding up again. The detective would prod him forward, not roughly, just as a sort of reminder to keep going.

"Why'd they put them *there*?" he asked. "Things that go in there are meant for fuel. That's what you came back for, to finish burning them, isn't it? Too late in the year to make a fire in the daytime without attracting attention."

"Listen. We were only married six weeks."

"What's that supposed to prove? Do you think there haven't been guys that got rid of their wives six *days* after they were married, or even six *hours*?"

"But those are fiends—monsters. *I* couldn't be one of them!"

And the pitiless answer was: "How do we know that? We can't tell, from the outside, what you're like on the inside. We're not X-ray machines."

They were up on the main floor again by now.

"Was she insured?" the detective questioned.

"Yes."

"You tell everything, don't you?"

"Because there's nothing to hide. I didn't just insure *her*, I insured us both. I took out twin policies, one on each of us. We were each other's beneficiaries. She wanted it that way."

"But you're here and she's not," the detective pointed out remorselessly.

They passed the dining-room entrance. Maybe it was the dishes still left on the table from that night that got to him. She came before him again, with her smiling crinkly eyes. He could see her carrying in a plate covered with a napkin. "Sit down there, mister, and don't look. I've got a surprise for you."

That finished him. That was a blow below the belt. He said, "You gotta let me alone a minute." And he slumped against the wall with his arm up over his face.

When he finally got over it, and it took some getting over, a sort of change had come over the detective. He said tonelessly, "Sit down a minute. Get your breath back and pull yourself together." He didn't sound like he meant that particularly, it was just an excuse.

He lighted a cigarette and then he threw the pack over at Bliss. Bliss let it slide off his thigh without bothering with it.

The detective said, "I've been a dick going on eight years

now, and I never saw a guy who could fake a spell like you just had, and make it so convincing." He paused, then went on: "The reason I'm saying this is, once you go in you stay in, after what we found here in the house tonight. And, then, you did come up to me outside of your own accord, but of course that could have been just self-preservation. So I'm listening, for just as long as it takes me to finish this cigarette. By the time I'm through, if you haven't been able to tell me anything that changes the looks of things around, away we go." And he took a puff and waited.

"There's nothing I can tell you that I haven't already told you. She walked out of here Tuesday night at supper time. Said she was going to her mother's. She never got there. I haven't seen her since. Now you fellows find the things I saw her leave in, stuffed into the furnace in the basement." He pinched the bridge of his nose and kept it pinched.

The detective took another slow pull at his cigarette. "You've been around to the morgue and the hospitals. So she hadn't had any accident. Her things are back here again. So it isn't just a straight disappearance, or amnesia, or anything like that. That means that whatever was done to her or with her, was done against her will. Since we've eliminated accident, suicide, voluntary and involuntary disappearance, that spells murder."

"Don't!" Bliss said.

"It's got to be done." The detective took another puff. "Let's get down to motive. Now, you already have one, and a damned fine one. You'll have to dig up one on the part of somebody else that'll be stronger than yours, if you expect to cancel it out."

"Who could want to hurt her? She was so lovely, she was so beautiful—"

"Sometimes it's dangerous for a girl to be too lovely, too beautiful. It drives a man out of his mind; the man that can't have her. Were there any?"

"You're talking about Smiles now," Bliss growled dangerously, tightening his fist.

"I'm talking about a *case*. A case of suspected murder. And to us cases aren't beautiful, aren't ugly, they're just punishable." He puffed again. "Did she turn anyone down to marry you?"

Bliss shook his head. "She once told me I was the first fellow she ever went with."

The detective took another puff at his cigarette. He looked at it, shifted his fingers back a little, then looked at Bliss. "I seldom smoke that far down," he warned him. "I'm giving you a break. There's one more drag left in it. Anyone else stand to gain anything, financially, by her death, outside of yourself?"

"No one I know of."

The detective took the last puff, dropped the butt, ground it out. "Well, let's go," he said. He fumbled under his coat, took out a pair of handcuffs. "Incidentally, what was her real name? I have to know when I bring you in."

"Teresa."

"Smiles was just your pet name for her, eh?" The detective seemed to be just talking aimlessly, to try to take the sting out of the pinch, keep Bliss's mind off the handcuffs.

"Yeah," Bliss said, holding out his wrist without being told to. "I was the first one called her that. She never liked to be called Teresa. Her mother was the one always stuck to that."

He jerked his wrist back in again.

"C'mon, don't get hard to handle," the detective growled, reaching out after it.

"Wait a minute," Bliss said excitedly, and stuck his hand behind his back. "Some things have been bothering me. You brought one of them back just then. I nearly had it. Let me look, before I lose it again. Let me look at that letter a minute that her mother sent her yesterday. It's here in my pocket."

He stripped it out of the envelope. *Smiles, dear,* it began.

He opened his mouth and looked at the other man. "That's funny. Her mother never called her anything but

Teresa. I know I'm right about that. How could she? It was my nickname. And I'd never seen her until last night and—and Smiles hadn't been home since we were married."

The detective, meanwhile, kept trying to snag his other hand—he was holding the letter in his left—and bring it around in front of him.

"Wait a minute, wait a minute," Bliss pleaded. "I've got one of those things now. There was like a hitch in the flow of conversation, an air pocket. She said, 'I'm Smiles' mother,' and he said, 'You're *Teresa's* mother,' like he was reminding her what she always called Smiles. Why should he have to remind her of what she always called Smiles herself?"

"And that's supposed to clear you of suspicion, because her mother picks up your nickname for your wife, after she's been talking to you on the phone two or three days in a row? Anyone would be liable to do that. She did it to sort of accommodate you. Didn't you ever hear of people doing that before? That's how nicknames spread."

"But she caught it *ahead of time*, before she heard me call it to her. This letter heading shows that. She didn't know Smiles had disappeared yet, when she sent this letter. Therefore she hadn't spoken to me yet."

"Well, then, she got it from the husband, or from your wife's own letters home."

"But she never used it before; she disliked it until now. She wrote Smiles and told her openly it sounded too much like the nickname of a chorus girl. I can prove it to you. I can show you. Wait a minute, whatever your name is. Won't you let me see if I can find some other letter from her, just to convince myself?"

My name is Stillman, and it's too small a matter to make any difference one way or the other. Now, come on Bliss; I've tried to be fair with you until now—"

"Nothing is too small a matter to be important. You're a detective; do I have to tell you that? It's the little things in life that count, never the big ones. The little ones go to make up the big ones. Why should she suddenly call her by a nickname she never used before and disapproved of? Wait, let me show you. There must be one of her old letters upstairs yet, left around in one of the bureau drawers. Just let me go up and hunt for it. It'll take just a minute."

Stillman went up with him, but Bliss could tell he was slowly souring on him. He hadn't changed over completely yet, but he was well under way. "I've taken all the stalling I'm going to from you," he muttered tight-lipped. "If I've got to crack down on you to get you out of here with me, I'll show you that I can do that, too."

Bliss was pawing through his wife's drawers meanwhile, head tensely lowered, knowing he had to beat his captor's change of mood to the punch, that in another thirty seconds at the most the slow-to-anger detective was going to yank him flat on the floor by the slack of the collar and drag him bodily out of the room after him.

He found one at last, almost when he'd given up hope. The same medium-blue ink, the same note paper. They hadn't corresponded with any great frequency, but they had corresponded regularly, about once every month or so.

"Here," he said relievedly, "here, see?" And he spread it out flat on the dresser top. Then he spread the one from his pocket alongside it, to compare. "See? 'Dearest Teresa.' What did I tell—"

He never finished it. They both saw it at once. It would have been hard to miss, the way he'd put both missives edge to edge. Bliss looked at the detective, then back at the dresser again.

Stillman was the first to put it into words. An expression of sudden concentration had come over his face. He elbowed Bliss a little aside, to get a better look. "See if you can dig up some more samples of her writing," he said slowly. "I'm not an expert, but, unless I miss my guess, these two letters weren't written by the same person."

Bliss didn't need to be told twice. He was frantically going through everything of Smiles' he could lay his hands on, all her keepsakes, mementos, accumulated belongings, scattering them around. He stopped as suddenly as he'd begun, and Stillman saw him standing there staring fixedly at something in one of the trinket boxes he had been plumbing through.

"What's the matter? Did you find some more?"

Bliss acted scared. His face was pale. "No, not writing," he said in a bated voice. "Something even— Look."

The detective's chin thrust over his shoulder. "Who are they?"

"That's evidently a snapshot of her and her mother, taken at a beach when she was a girl. I've never seen it before, but—"

"How do you know it's her mother? It could be some other woman, a friend of the family's."

Bliss had turned it over right while he was speaking. On the back, in schoolgirlish handwriting, was the notation: *Mamma and I, at Sea Crest, 19—*

Bliss reversed it again, right side forward.

"Well, what're you acting so scared about?" Stillman demanded impatiently. "You look like you've seen a ghost."

"Because this woman on the snapshot isn't the same woman I spoke to as her mother up at Denby tonight!"

"Now, wait a minute; hold your horses. You admit yourself you had never set eyes on her before until tonight; eight years is eight years. She's in a bathing-suit in this snapshot. She may have dyed or bleached her hair since, or it may have turned gray on her."

"That has nothing to do with it! I'm not looking at her hair or her clothes. The whole shape of her face is different. The bone structure is different. The features are different. This woman has a broad, round face. The one in Denby has a long, oval one. I tell you, it's not the same woman at all!"

"Gimme that, and gimme those." Stillman pocketed letters and snapshot. "Come on downstairs. I think I'll smoke another cigarette." His way of saying: "You've got yourself a reprieve."

When they were below again, he sat down, with a misleading air of leisure. "Gimme your wife's family background, as much of it as you can, as much of it as she told you."

"Smiles was down here on her own when I met her. Her own father died when she was a kid, and left them comfortably well off, with their own house up in—"

"Denby?"

"No, it was some other place; I can't think of it offhand. While she was still a youngster, her mother gave Smiles her whole time and attention. But when Smiles had finished her schooling, about two years ago, the mother was still an attractive woman, young for her years, lively, good-hearted. It was only natural that she should marry again. Smiles didn't resent that; she'd expected her to. When the mother fell for this mason, Joe Alden, whom she first met when they were having some repairs made to the house, Smiles tried to like him. He'd been a good man in his line, too, but she couldn't help noticing that after he married her mother, he stopped dead, never did a stroke of work from then on; pretending he couldn't find any—when she knew for a fact that there was work to be had. That was the first thing she didn't like. Maybe he sensed she was onto him, but anyway they didn't rub well together. For her mother's sake, to avoid trouble, she decided to clear out, so her mother wouldn't have to choose between them. She was so diplomatic about it, though, that her mother never guessed what the real reason was.

"She came on down here, and not long ago Alden and her mother sold their own house and moved to a new one in Denby. Smiles said she supposed he did it to get away from the gossipy neighbors as much as anything else; they were probably beginning to criticize him for not at least making a stab at getting a job after he was once married."

"Did they come down when you married Smiles?"

"No. Smiles didn't notify them ahead; just sent a wire of announcement the day we were married. Her mother had been in poor health, and she was afraid the trip down would be more than she could stand. Well, there's the background."

"Nothing much there to dig into, at first sight."

"There never is, anywhere—at first sight," Bliss let him know. "Listen, Stillman. I'm going back up there again. Whatever's wrong is up at that end, not at this."

"I was detailed here to bring you in for questioning, you know." But he didn't move.

"Suppose I hadn't gone up to you outside in the street just now. Suppose I hadn't shown up around here for, say, another eight or ten hours. Can't you give me those extra hours? Come up there with me, never leave me out of your sight, put the bracelet on me, do anything you want, but at least let me go up there once more and confront those people. If you lock me up down at this end, then I've lost her sure as anything. I'll never find out what became of her— and you won't either. Something bothered me up there. A whole lot of things bothered me up there, but I've only cleared up one of them so far. Let me take a crack at the rest.

"You don't want much," Stillman said grudgingly. "D'ya know what can happen to me for stepping out of line like that? D'ya know I can be broken for anything like that?"

"You mean you're ready to ignore the discrepancy in handwriting in those two letters, and my assurance that there's someone up there that doesn't match the woman on that snapshot?"

"No, naturally not; I'm going to let my lieutenant know about both those things."

"And by that time it'll be too late. It's already three days since she's been gone."

"Tell you what," Stillman said. "I'll make a deal with you. We'll start out for headquarters now, and on the way we'll stop in at that bus terminal. If I can find any evidence, the slightest shred, that she started for Denby that night, I'll go up there with you. If not, we go over to headquarters."

All Bliss said was: "I know you'll find out she did leave."

Stillman took him without handcuffing him, merely remarking, "If you try anything, you'll be the loser, not me."

The ticket-seller again went as far as he had with Bliss the time before, but still couldn't go any further than that. "Yeah, she bought a ticket for as far as the money she had on her would take her, but I can't remember where it was to."

"Which don't prove she ever hit Denby," Stillman grunted.

"Tackle the bus driver," Bliss pleaded. "No. 27. I know he was holding out on me. I could tell by the way he acted. She rode with him, all right, but for some reason he was cagey about saying so."

But they were out of luck. No. 27 was up at the other end, due to bring the cityward bus in the following afternoon.

Stillman was already trying to steer his charge out of the place and on his way over to headquarters, but Bliss wouldn't give up. "There must be someone around here that saw her get on that night. One of the attendants, one of the concessionaires that are around here every night. Maybe she checked her bag, maybe she drank a cup of coffee at the counter."

She hadn't checked her bag; the checkroom attendant couldn't remember anyone like her. She hadn't stopped at the lunch counter, either; neither could the counterman recall her. Nor the Negro that shined shoes. They even interrogated the matron of the restroom, when she happened to appear outside the door briefly. No, she hadn't noticed anyone like that, either.

"All right, come on," Stillman said, hooking his arm around Bliss's.

"One more spin. How about him, over there, behind the magazine stand?"

Stillman only gave in because it happened to be near the exit; they had to pass it on their way out.

And it broke! The fog lifted, if only momentarily, for the first time since the previous Tuesday night. "Sure I do," the vendor said readily. "How could I help remembering? She came up to me in such a funny way. She said, 'I have exactly one dime left, which I overlooked when I was buying my ticket because it slipped to the bottom of my handbag. Let me have a magazine.' Naturally, I asked her which one she wanted. 'I don't care,' she said, 'so long as it lasts until I get off the bus. I want to be sure my mind is taken up.' Well, I've been doing business here for years, and it's gotten so I can clock the various stops. I mean, if they're riding a long distance, I give them a good thick magazine; if they're riding a short distance, I give them a skinny one. I gave her one for a medium distance—Denby; that was where she told me she was going."

All Stillman said was: "Come on over to the window while I get our tickets."

Bliss didn't say "Thanks." He didn't say anything. He didn't have to. The grateful look he gave the detective spoke for itself.

"Two to Denby, round," Stillman told the ticket-seller. It was too late for the morning bus; the next one left in the early afternoon.

As they turned from the window, Bliss wondered aloud:

"Still and all, why was that driver so reluctant to admit she rode on the bus with him that night? And the ticket man claims she didn't buy a ticket to Denby, but to some point short of there."

"It's easy to see what it adds up to," Stillman told him. "She had a ticket for only part of the distance. She coaxed the driver into letting her ride the rest of the way to Denby. Probably explained her plight to him, and he felt sorry for her. That explains his reluctance to let you think she was on the bus at all. He must have thought you were a company spotter and naturally what he did would be against the regulations."

Tucking away the tickets in his inside coat pocket, the

detective stood there a moment or two undecidedly. Then he said, "We may as well go back to your house. I might be able to turn up something else while we're waiting, and you can catch a nap. And, too, I'm going to call in, see if I can still make this detour up there and back legitimate while I'm about it."

When they got back to his house Bliss, exhausted, fell asleep in the bedroom. He remained oblivious to everything until the detective woke him up a half hour before bus time.

"Any luck?" Bliss asked him, shrugging into his coat.

"Nope, nothing more," Stillman said. Then he announced, "I've given my word to my lieutenant I'll show up at headquarters and have you with me, no later than nine tomorrow morning. He doesn't know you're with me right now; I let him think I got a tip where I could lay my hands on you. Leaving now, we will get up there around sunset, and we'll have to take the night bus back. That gives us only a few hours up there to see if we can find any trace of her. Pretty tight squeeze, if you ask me."

They boarded the bus together and sat down in one of the back seats. They didn't talk much during the long, monotonous ride up.

"Better take another snooze while you've got the chance," Stillman said.

Bliss thought he wouldn't be able to again, but, little by little, sheer physical exhaustion, combined with the lulling motion of the bus, overcame him and he dropped off.

It seemed like only five minutes later that Stillman shook him by the shoulder, rousing him. The sun was low in the west; he'd slept through nearly the entire trip. "Snap out of it, Bliss; we get off in another couple of minutes, right on time."

"I dreamed about her," Bliss said dully. "I dreamed she was in some kind of danger, needed me bad. She kept calling to me, 'Ed! Hurry up, Ed!' "

Stillman dropped his eyes. "I heard you say her name twice in your sleep: 'Smiles, Smiles,' " he remarked quietly.

"Damned if you act like any guilty man I ever had in my custody before. Even in your sleep you sound like you were innocent."

"Denby!" the driver called out.

As the bus pulled away and left them behind at the crossroads, Stillman said, "Now that we're up here, let's have an understanding with each other. I don't want to haul you around on the end of a handcuff with me, but my job is at stake; I've got to be sure that you're still with me when I start back."

"Would my word of honor that I won't try to give you the slip while we're up here be worth anything to you?"

Stillman looked at him square in the eye. "Is it worth anything to *you*?"

"It's about all I've got. I know I've never broken it."

Stillman nodded slowly. "I think maybe it'll be worth taking a chance on. All right, let me have it."

They shook hands solemnly.

Dusk was rapidly falling by now; the sun was already gone from sight and its afterglow fading out.

"Come on, let's get out to their place," Bliss said impatiently.

"Let's do a little inquiring around first. Remember, we have no evidence so far that she actually got off the bus here at all, let alone reached their house. Just her buying that magazine and saying she was coming here is no proof in itself. Now, let's see, she gets off in the middle of the night at this sleeping hamlet. Would she know the way out to their house, or would she have to ask someone?"

"She'd have to ask. Remember, I told you they moved here *after* Smiles had already left home. This would have been her first trip up here."

"Well, that ought to cinch it for us, if she couldn't get out there without asking directions. Let's try our luck at that filling-station first; it would probably have been the only thing open any more at the hour she came."

The single attendant on duty came out, said, "Yes,

gents?"

"Look," Stillman began. "The traffic to and from here isn't exactly heavy, so this shouldn't be too hard. Think back to Tuesday night, the last bus north. Did you see anyone get off it?"

"I don't have to see 'em get off; I got a sure-fire way of telling whether anyone gets off or not."

"What's that?"

"Anyone that does get off, at least anyone that's a stranger here, never fails to stop by me and ask their way. That's as far as the last bus is concerned. The store is closed before then. And no one asked their way of me Tuesday night, so I figure no strangers got off."

"This don't look so good," murmured Stillman in an aside to Bliss. Then he asked the attendant, "Did you hear it go by at all? You must have, it's so quiet here."

"Yeah, sure, I did. It was right on time, too."

"Then you could tell if it stopped to let anyone down or went straight through without stopping, couldn't you?"

"Yeah, usually I can," was the disappointing answer. "But just that night, at that particular time, I was doing some repair work on a guy's car, trying to hammer out a bent fender for him, and my own noise drowned it out. As long as no one stopped by, though, I'm pretty sure it never stopped."

"Damn it," Stillman growled, as they turned away, "she couldn't have been more unseen if she was a ghost!"

After they were out of earshot of the filling-station attendant, Bliss said, "If Alden, for instance, had known she was coming and waited to meet her at the bus, that would do away with her having to ask anyone for directions. She may have telephoned ahead, or sent a wire up."

"If she didn't even have enough money to buy a ticket all the way, she certainly wouldn't have been able to make a toll call. Anyway, if we accept that theory, that means we're implicating them directly in her disappearance, and we have no evidence so far to support that. Remember, she may have met with foul play right here in Denby, along the road to their house, without ever having reached it."

It was fully dark by the time they rounded the bend in the road and came in sight of that last house of all, with the low brick wall in front of it. This time not a patch of light showed from any of the windows, upstairs or down, and yet it was earlier in the evening than when Bliss himself had arrived.

"Hello?" the detective said. "Looks like nobody's home."

They turned in under the willow arch, rang the bell, and waited. Stillman pummeled the door and they waited some more. This was just perfunctory, however; it had been obvious to the two of them from the moment they first looked at the place that no one was in.

"Well, come on. What're we waiting for?" Bliss demanded. "I can get in one of the windows without any trouble."

Stillman laid a restraining hand on his arm. "No, you don't; that's breaking and entering. And I'm out of jurisdiction up here to begin with. We'll have to go back and dig up the local law; maybe I can talk him into putting the seal of official approval on it. Let's see if we can tell anything from the outside, first. I may be able to shine my torch in through one of the windows."

He clicked it on, made a white puddle against the front of the house, walked slowly in the wake of that as it moved along until it leaped in through one of the black window embrasures. They both edged up until their noses were nearly pressed flat against the glass, trying to peer through. It wouldn't work. The blinds were not down, but the closely webbed net curtains that hung down inside of the panes effectively parried its rays. They coursed slowly along the side of the house, trying it at window after window, each time with the same results.

Stillman turned away finally, but left his torch on. He splashed it up and down the short length of private dirt lane that ran beside the house, from the corrugated tin shack at the back that served Alden as a garage to the public highway

in front. He motioned Bliss back as the latter started to step
out onto it. "Stay off here a minute. I want to see if I can
find out something from these tire prints their car left. See
'em?"

It would have been hard not to. The road past the house
was macadamized, but there was a border of soft, powdery
dust along the side of it, as with most rural roads. "I want to
see if I can make out which way they turned," Stillman explained, strewing his beam of light along them and following
offside. "If they went in to the city, to offer their coopera-
tion to us down there, that would take them off to the right;
no other way they could turn from here. If they turned to
the left, up that way, it was definitely a lam, and it changes
the looks of things all around."

The beam of his light, coursing along the prints like
quicksilver in a channel, started to curve around *toward the
right* as it followed them up out of sight on the hard-surfaced
road. There was his answer.

He turned aimlessly back along them, light still on. He
stopped parallel to the corner of the house, strengthened the
beam's focus by bringing the torch down closer to the
ground. "Here's something else," Bliss heard him say.
"Funny how you can notice every little thing in this fine
floury dust. His front left tire had a patch on it, and a bad
one, too. See it? You can tell just what they did. Alden evidently ran the car out of the shed alone, ahead of his wife.
She got in here at the side of the house, to save time, instead
of going out the front way; they were going down the road
the other way, anyway. His wheel came to rest with the
patch squarely under it. That's why it shows so plain in this
one place. Then he took his brake off and the car coasted
back a little with the tilt of the ground. When he came forward again, the position of his wheel diverged a little, missed
erasing its own former imprint. Bet they have trouble with
that before the night's over."

He spoke as though it were just a trivial detail. But is anything, Bliss was to ask himself later, a trivial detail?

"Come on," Stillman concluded, pocketing his light, "let's go get the law and see what it looks like on the inside."

The constable's name was Cochrane, and they finally located him at his own home. "Evening," Stillman introduced himself, "I'm Stillman of the city police. I was wondering if there's some way we could get a look inside that Alden house. Their—er—stepdaughter has disappeared down in the city; she was supposed to have started for here, and this is just a routine check. Nothing against them. They seem to be out, and we have to make the next bus back."

Cochrane plucked at his throat judiciously. "Well, now, I guess I can accommodate you, as long as it's done in my presence. I'm the law around here, and if they've got nothing to hide, there's no reason why they should object. I'll drive ye back in my car. This feller here your subordinate, I s'pose?"

Stillman said, "Um," noncommittally, favored Bliss with a nudge. The constable would have probably balked at letting a man already wanted by the police into these people's house, they both knew, even if he was accompanied by a bona fide detective.

He stopped off at his office first to get a master key, came back with the remark: "This ought to do the trick." They were back at the Alden place once more inside of ten minutes, all told, from the time they had first left it.

Cochrane favored them with a sly grimace as they got out and went up to the house. "I'm sort of glad you fellers asked me to do this, at that. Fact is, we've all been curious about them folks ourselves hereabouts for a long time past. Kind of unsociable; keep to themselves a lot. This is as good a time as any to see if they got any skeletons in the closet."

Bliss shuddered involuntarily at the expression.

The constable's master key opened the door without any great difficulty, and the three of them went in.

They looked in every room in the place from top to bottom, and in every closet of every room, and not one of the "skeletons" the constable had spoken of turned up, either allegorical or literal. There wasn't anything out of the way, and nothing to show that anything had ever been out of the way, in this house.

In the basement, when they reached it, were a couple of sagging, half-empty bags of cement in one corner, and pinkish traces of brick dust and brick grit on the floor, but that was easily accounted for. "Left over from when he was putting up that wall along the roadside a while back, I guess," murmured Cochrane.

They turned and went upstairs again. The only other discovery of any sort they made was not of a guilty nature, but simply an indication of how long ago the occupants had left. Stillman happened to knuckle a coffeepot standing on the kitchen range, and it was still faintly warm from the residue of liquid left in it.

"They must have only just left before we got here," he said to Bliss. "Missed them just by minutes."

"Funny; why did they wait until after dark to start on a long trip like that? Why didn't they leave sooner?"

"That don't convict them of anything, just the same," Stillman maintained obdurately. "We haven't turned up a shred of evidence that your wife ever saw the inside of this house. Don't try to get around that."

The local officer, meanwhile, had gone outside to put some water in his car. "Close the door good after you as you come out," he called out to them.

They were already at the door, but Bliss unaccountably turned and went back inside again. When Stillman followed him a moment later, he was sitting there in the living-room raking his fingers perplexedly through his hair.

"Come on," the detective said, as considerately as he could, "let's get going. He's waiting for us."

Bliss looked up at him helplessly. "Don't you get it? Doesn't this room bother you?"

Stillman looked around vaguely. "No. In what way? What's wrong with it? To me it seems clean, well kept, and comfortable. All you could ask for."

"There's something about it annoys me. I feel ill at ease in it. It's not *restful,* for some reason. And I have a peculiar feeling that if I could figure out *why* it isn't restful, it would help to partly clear up this mystery about Smiles."

Stillman sliced the edge of his hand at him scornfully. "Now you're beginning to talk plain crazy, Bliss. You say this room isn't restful. The room has nothing to do with it. It's you. You're all tense, jittery, about your wife. Your nerves are on edge, frayed to the breaking point. That's why the room don't seem restful to you. Naturally it don't. No room would."

Bliss kept shaking his head baffledly. "No. No. That may sound plausible, but I know that isn't it. It's not *me,* it's the room itself. I'll admit I'm all keyed up, but I noticed it already the other night when I wasn't half so keyed up. Another thing: I don't get it in any of the other rooms in this house; I only get it in here."

"I don't like the way you're talking; I think you're starting to crack up under the strain," Stillman let him know, but he hung around in the doorway for a few minutes, watching him curiously, while Bliss sat there motionless, clasped hands hanging from the back of his neck now.

"Did you get it yet?"

Bliss raised his head, shook it mutely, chewing the corner of his mouth. "It's one of those things; when you try too hard for it, it escapes you altogether. It's only when you're sort of not thinking about it that you notice it. The harder I try to pin it down, the more elusive it becomes."

"Sure," said Stillman with a look of sympathetic concern, "and if you sit around in here brooding about it much more, I'll be taking you back with me in a straitjacket. Come on, we've only got ten more minutes to make that bus."

Bliss got reluctantly to his feet. "There it goes," he said. "I'll never get it now."

"Ah, you talk like these guys that keep trying to communicate with spirits through a ouija board," Stillman let him know, locking up the front door after them. "The whole thing was a wild-goose chase."

"No, it wasn't."

"Well, what'd we get out of it?"

"Nothing. But that doesn't mean it isn't around here waiting to be seen. It's just that we've missed seeing it, whatever it is."

"There's not a sign of her around that house. Not a sign of her ever having been there. Not a sign of violence."

"And I know that, by going away from here, we're turning our backs on whatever there is to be learned about what became of her. We'll never find out at the other end, in the city. I nearly had it, too, when I was sitting in there. Just as I was about to get it, it would slip away from me again. Talk about torture!"

Stillman lost his temper. "Will you lay off that room! If there was anything the matter with it, I'd notice it as well as you. My eyes are just as good, my brains are just as good. What's the difference between you and me?" The question was only rhetorical.

"You're a detective and I'm an architect," Bliss said inattentively, answering it as asked.

"Are you fellows going to stand there arguing all night?" the constable called from the other side of the wall.

They went out and got into the open car, started off. Bliss felt like groaning: "Good-bye, Smiles." Just as they reached the turn of the road that would have swept the house out of sight once they rounded it, Stillman happened to glance back for no particular reason, at almost the very last possible moment that it could still be seen in a straight line behind them.

"Hold it," he ejaculated, thumbing a slim bar of light narrowed by perspective. "We left the lights on in that last room we were in."

The constable braked promptly. "Have to go back and turn them off, or they'll—"

"We haven't time now, we'll miss the bus," Stillman cut in. "It's due in six more minutes. Drive us down to the crossroads first, and then you come back afterward and put them out yourself."

"No!" Bliss cried out wildly, jumping to his feet. "This has a meaning to it! I'm not passing this up! I want another look at those lights; they're asking me to, they're begging me to!" Before either one of them could stop him, he had jumped down from the side of the car without bothering to unlatch the door. He started to run back up the road, deaf to Stillman's shouts and imprecations.

"Come back here, you welsher! You gave me your word of honor!"

A moment later the detective's feet hit the ground and he started after his prisoner. But Bliss had already turned in through the opening in the wall, was flinging himself bodily against the door, without waiting for any master key this time. The infuriated detective caught him by the shoulder, swung him violently around, when he had reached him.

"Take your hands off me!" Bliss said hoarsely. "I'm going to get in there!"

Stillman swung at him and missed. Instead of returning the blow, Bliss threw his whole weight against the door for the last time. There was a rendering and splintering of wood, and it shot inward, leaving the whole lock intact against the frame. Bliss went flailing downward on his face into the hallway. He scrambled erect, reached the inner doorway, put his hand inside, and put the lights out without looking into the room.

"It's when they go on that counts," he panted.

The only reason Stillman wasn't grappling with him was that he couldn't locate him for a minute in the dark. The switch clicked a second time. Light flashed from the dazzlingly calcimined ceiling. Bliss was standing directly in the middle of the opening as it did so, just as he had been the first night.

Stillman was down the hall a few steps, couldn't see his face for a minute. "Well?" he asked.

Bliss turned to him without saying anything. The look on

his face answered for him. He'd gotten what he wanted.

"Why, they're not in the center of the ceiling! They're offside. That's what made them seem glaring, unexpected. They took my eyes by surprise. I've got professionally trained eyes, remember. They didn't go on where I expected them to, but a little farther over. And now that I have that much, I have it all." He gripped Stillman excitedly by the biceps. "Now I see what's wrong with the room. Now I see why I found it so unrestful. It's out of true."

"What?"

"Out of proportion. Look. Look at that window. It's not in the center of that wall. And d'you see how cleverly they've tried to cover the discrepancy? A thin, skinny, up-and-down picture on the short side; a big, wide, fat one on the longer side. That creates an optical illusion, makes both sides seem even. Now come over here and look this way." He pulled the detective in after him, turned him around by the shoulder. "Sure, same thing with the door frame; that's not dead center, either. But the door opens inward into the room, swings to that short side and partly screens it, throws a shadow over it, so that takes care of that. What else? What else?"

He kept pivoting feverishly, sweeping his glance around on all sides. "Oh, sure, the rug. I was sitting here and I dropped some ashes and looked down at the floor. See what bothered me about that? Again there's an unbalance. See the margin of polished woodwork running around on three sides of it? And on the fourth side it runs right smack up against the baseboard of the wall. Your eye wants proportion, symmetry; it's got to have it in all things. If it doesn't get it, it's uncomfortable. It wants that dark strip of woodwork on all *four* sides, or else the rug should touch all four baseboards, like a carpet—"

He was talking slower and slower, like a record that's running down. Some sort of tension was mounting in him, gripping him, Stillman could tell by looking at him. He panted the last few words out, as if it took all his strength to produce them, and then his voice died away altogether, without a period.

"What're you getting so white around the gills for?" the detective demanded. "Suppose the room is lopsided, what then? Your face is turning all green—"

Bliss had to grab him by the shoulder for a minute for support. His voice was all furry with dawning horror. "Because—because—don't you see what it means? Don't you see *why* it's that way? One of these walls is a dummy wall, built out *in front* of the real one." His eyes were dilated with unbelieving horror. He clawed insensately at his own hair. "It all hangs together so damnably! He was a mason before he married her mother; I told you that. The storekeeper down at the crossroads said that Alden built a low brick wall in front of the house, 'just to keep in practice,' he guessed. No reason for it. It wasn't high enough for privacy, it didn't even run around all four sides of the plot.

"He didn't build it just to keep in practice! He did it to get the bricks in here from the contractor. More than he needed. He put it up just to have an excuse to order them. Who's going to count— Don't stand there! Get an ax, a crowbar; help me break this thing down! Don't you see what this dummy wall is for? Don't you see what we'll find—"

The detective had been slower in grasping it, but he finally got it, too. His own face went gray. "Which one is it?"

"It must be on this side, the side that's the shortest distance from the window, door, and light fixture." Bliss rushed up to it, began to pound it with his clenched fists, up and down, sounding it out. Sweat flew literally off his face like raindrops in a stiff wind.

The detective bolted out of the room, sent an excited yell at the open front door:

"Cochrane! Come in here, give us a hand, bring tools!"

Between the two of them they dug up a hatchet, a crowbar, cold chisel, and bung starter. "That wall," the detective explained tersely for the constable's benefit, without going into details. Cochrane didn't argue; one look at both their faces must have told him that some unspeakable horror was on the way to revelation.

Bliss was leaning sideways against it by now, perfectly still, head lowered almost as though he were trying to hear something through it. He wasn't. His head was lowered with the affliction of discovery. "I've found it," he said stifledly. "I've found—the place. Listen." He pounded once or twice. There was the flat impact of solidity. He moved farther over, pounded again. This time there was the deeper resonance of a partly, or only imperfectly, filled orifice. "Half bricks, with a hollow behind them. Elsewhere, whole bricks, mortar behind them."

Stillman stripped his coat off, spit on his hands. "Better get out of the room—in case you're right," he suggested, flying at it with the hatchet, to knock off the plaster. "Wait outside the door; we'll call you—"

"No! I've got to know, I've got to see. Three of us are quicker than two." And he began chipping off the plaster coating with the cutting edge of the chisel. Cochrane cracked it for them with the bung starter. A cloud of dust hovered about them while they hacked away. Finally, they had laid bare an upright, *coffin-shaped* segment of pinkish-white brickwork in the plaster finish of the wall.

They started driving the chisel in between the interstices of the brick ends, Stillman steadying it, Cochrane driving it home with the bung starter. They changed to the crowbar, started to work that as a lever, when they'd pierced a big enough space.

"Look out. One of them's working out."

A fragment of brick ricocheted halfway across the room, dropped with a thud. A second one followed. A third. Bliss started to claw at the opening with his bare nails, to enlarge it faster.

"You're only impeding us; we can get at it faster this way," Stillman said, pushing him aside. A gray fill of imperfectly dried clayey mortar was being laid bare. It was only a shell; flakes of it, like dried mud, had begun dropping off and out, some of their own weight, others with the impact of their blows, long before they had opened more than a "window" in the brickwork façade.

"Get back," Stillman ordered. His purpose was to protect Bliss from the full impact of discovery that was about to ensue.

Bliss obeyed him at last, staggered over to the other end of the room, stood there with his back to them as if he were looking out the window. Only the window was farther over. A spasmodic shiver went down his back every so often. He could hear the pops and thuds as brick fragments continued to drop out of the wall under the others' efforts, then a sudden engulfing silence.

He turned his head just in time to see them lowering something from the niche in the wall. An upright something. A rigid, mummified, columnar something that resembled nothing so much as a log covered with mortar. The scant remainder of bricks that still held it fast below, down toward the floor, shattered, spilled down in a little freshet as they wrenched it free. A haze of kindly concealing dust veiled them from him. For a minute or two they were just white shadows working over something, and then they had this thing lying on the floor. A truncated thing without any human attributes whatever, like the mold around a cast metal statue—but with a core that was something else again.

"Get out of here, Bliss," Stillman growled. "This is no place for you!"

Wild horses couldn't have dragged Bliss away. He was numbed beyond feeling now, anyway. The whole scene had been one that could never again be forgotten by a man who had once lived through it.

"Not with that" he protested, as he saw the crouching Stillman flick open the large blade of a penknife.

"It's the only thing I *can* use! Go out and get us some water, see if we can soften this stuff up a little, dissolve it."

When Bliss came back with a pail of it, Stillman was working away cautiously at one end of the mound, shaving a little with the knife blade, probing and testing with his fingers. He desisted suddenly, flashed the constable a mutely eloquent look, shifted up to the opposite end. Bliss, staring with glazed eyes, saw a stubby bluish-black wedge peering through where he had been working—the tip of a woman's shoe.

"Upside down at that," grunted Cochrane, trying not to let Bliss overhear him. The latter's teeth were chattering with nervous shock.

"I told you to get out of here!" Stillman flared for the third and last time. "Your face is driving me crazy!" With as little effect as before.

Fine wires seemed to hold some of it together, even after he had pared it with the knife blade. He wet the palms of his hands in the pail of water, kneaded and crumbled it between them in those places. What had seemed like stiff wires were strands of human hair.

"That's enough," he said finally in a sick voice. "There's someone there; that's all I wanted to be sure of. I don't know how to go about the rest of it, much; an expert'll have to attend to that."

"Them devils," growled Cochrane deep in his throat.

Bliss suddenly toppled down between them, so abruptly they both thought he had fainted for a minute. "Stillman!" he said in a low throbbing voice. He was almost leaning across the thing. "These wisps of hair— Look! They show through dark, bluish-black! *She was blond!* Like an angel. It's somebody else!"

Stillman nodded, held his forehead dazedly. "Sure, it must be. I don't have to go by that; d'you know what should have told me from the beginning? Your wife's only been missing since Tuesday night, three days ago. The condition of the mortar shows plainly that this job's been up for weeks past. Why, the paint on the outside of the wall would have hardly been dry yet, let alone the fill in back of it. Apart from that, it would have been humanly impossible to put up such a job single-handed in three days. We both lost our heads; it shows you it doesn't pay to get excited.

"It's the mother, that's who it is. There's your answer for the discrepancy in the handwriting on the two notes, the snapshot, and that business about the nickname that puzzled you. Come on, stand up and lean on me, we're going to find out where he keeps his liquor. You need a drink if a man ever did!"

They found some in a cupboard out in the kitchen, sat down for a minute. Bliss looked as if he'd been pulled through a knothole. The constable had gone out on wobbly legs to get a breath of fresh air.

Bliss put the bottle down and started to look alive again.

"I think I'll have a gulp myself," Stillman said. "I'm not a drinking man, but that was one of the nastiest jobs in there just now I've ever been called on to participate in."

The constable rejoined them, his face still slightly greenish. He had a drink, too.

"How many of them were there when they first moved in here?" Stillman asked him.

"Only two. Only him and his wife, from first to last."

"Then you never saw her; they hid her from sight, that's all."

"They've been kind of standoffish; no one's ever been inside the place until tonight."

"It's her, all right, the real mother," Bliss said, as soon as he'd gotten his mental equilibrium back. "I don't have to see the face; I know I'm right. No, no more. I'm O.K. now, and I want to be able to think clearly. Don't you touch any more of it, either, Still. That's who it must be. Don't you see how the whole thing hangs together? Smiles *did* show up here Tuesday night, or rather in the early hours of Wednesday morning; I'm surer than ever of it now. You asked me, back at my house, for a motive that would overshadow that possible insurance one of mine. Well, here it is; this is it. She was the last one they expected to see, so soon after her own marriage to me. She walked in here and found an impostor in the place of her own mother, a stranger impersonating her. They had to shut her up quick, keep her from raising an alarm. There's your motive as far as Smiles is concerned."

"And it's a wow," concurred Stillman heartily. "The thing is, what've they done with her, where is she? We're no better off than before. She's not around here; we've cased the place from cellar to attic. Unless there's another of those trick walls that we've missed spotting."

"You're forgetting that what you said about the first one still goes. There hasn't been time enough to rig up anything that elaborate."

"I shouldn't have taken that drink," confessed Stillman.

"I'm convinced she was here, though, as late as Thursday night, and still alive in the place. Another of those tantalizing things just came back to me. There was a knock on one of the water pipes somewhere; I couldn't tell if it was upstairs or down. I bet she was tied up someplace, the whole time I was sitting here."

"Did you hear one or more than one?"

"Just one. The woman got right up and went out, I noticed, giving an excuse about getting a fresh handkerchief. They probably had her doped, or under some sedative."

"That's then, but now?"

"There's a lot of earth around outside, acres of it, miles of it," Cochrane put in morbidly.

"No, now wait a minute," Stillman interjected. "Let's get this straight. If their object was just to make her disappear, clean vanish, as in the mother's case, that would be one thing. Then I'm afraid we might find her lying somewhere around in that earth you speak of. But you're forgetting that her clothes turned up in your own furnace at home, Bliss— showing they didn't want her to disappear; they wanted to pin her death definitely on you."

"Why?"

"Self-preservation, pure and simple. With a straight disappearance, the investigation would have never been closed. In the end it might have been directed up this way, resulted in unearthing the first murder, just as we did tonight. Pin-ning it on you would have not only obviated that risk, but eliminated you as well—cleaned the slate for them. A second murder to safeguard the first, a legal execution to clinch the second. But—to pin it successfully on you, that body has to show up down around where you are, and not up here at all. The clothes were a forerunner of it."

"But would they risk taking her back to my place, knowing it was likely to be watched by you fellows, once they had denounced me to you themselves? That would be like sticking their own heads in a noose. They might know it would be kept under surveillance."

"No, it wouldn't have been. You see, your accidental switch to that hitchhike from the bus resulted in two things going wrong. We not only went out to your house to look for you when you didn't show up at the terminal, but, by going out there, we found the clothes in the furnace sooner than they wanted us to. I don't believe they were meant to be found until—the body was also in position."

"Then why make two trips, instead of just one? Why not take poor Smiles at the same time they took her clothes?"

"He had to make a fast trip in, the first time, to beat that bus. They may have felt it was too risky to take her along then. He also had to familiarize himself with your premises, find some way of getting in, find out if the whole thing was feasible or not before going ahead with it. They felt their call to us—it wasn't an accusation at all, by the way, but simply a request that we investigate—would get you out of the way, clear the coast for them. They expected you to be held and questioned for twenty-four, forty-eight hours, straight. They thought they'd given themselves a wide enough margin of safety. But your failure to take the bus telescoped it."

Bliss rose abruptly. "Do you think she's—yet?" He couldn't bring himself to mention the word.

"It stands to reason that they'd be foolish to do it until the last possible moment. That would increase the risk of transporting her a hundredfold. And they'd be crazy to do it anywhere else but on the exact spot where they intend her to be found eventually. Otherwise, it would be too easy for us to reconstruct the fact that she was killed somewhere else and taken there afterward."

"Then the chances are she was still alive when they left here with her! There may still be time even now; she may still be alive! What are we sitting here like this for?"

They both bolted out together, but Bliss made for the front door, Stillman headed for the phone in the hall.

"What're you doing that for?"

"Phone in an alarm to city headquarters. How else can we hope to save her? Have them throw a cordon around your house—"

Bliss pulled the instrument out of his hands. "Don't! You'll only be killing her quicker that way! If we frighten them off, we'll never save her. They'll lose their heads, kill her anywhere and drop her off just to get rid of her. This way, at least we know it'll be in or somewhere around my house."

"But, man, do you realize the head start they've had?"

"We only missed them by five or ten minutes. Remember that coffeepot on the stove?"

"Even so, even with a State police escort, I doubt if we can get in under a couple of hours."

"And I say that we've got to take the chance! You noticed their tire treads before. He has a walloping bad patch, and he's never going to make that bad stretch on the road with it. I saw his car last night when it raced past, and he had no spares up. There's no gas station for miles around there. All that will cut down their head start."

"You're willing to gamble your wife's life against a flat tire?"

"There isn't anything else I *can* do. I'm convinced if you send an alarm ahead and have a dragnet thrown around my house, they'll scent it and simply shy away from there and go off someplace else with her where we *won't* be able to get to her in time, because we won't know where it is. Come on, we could be miles away already, for the time we've wasted talking."

"All right," snapped the detective, "we'll play it your way! Is this car of yours any good?" he asked Cochrane, hopping in.

"Fastest thing in these parts," said the constable grimly, slithering under the wheel.

"Well, you know what you've got to do with it: cut down their head start to nothing flat, less than nothing; you've got to get us there five minutes to the good."

"Just get down low in your seats and hang onto your back teeth," promised Cochrane. "What we just turned up in there happened in my jurisdiction, don't forget—and the law of the land gives this road to us tonight!"

It was an incredible ride; incredible for the fact that they stayed right side up on the surface of the road at all. The speedometer needle clung to stratospheric heights throughout. The scenery was just a blurred hiss on both sides of them. The wind pressure stung the pupils of their eyes to the point where they could barely hold them open. The constable, luckily, used glasses for reading and had happened to have them about him when they started. He put them on simply in order to make sure of staying on the road at all.

They had to take the bad stretch at a slower speed in sheer self-defense, in order not to have the same thing happen to them that they were counting on having happened to the Alden car. An intact tire could possibly get over it unharmed, but one that was already defective was almost sure to go out.

"Wouldn't you think he'd have remembered about this from passing over it last night, and taken precautions?" Stillman yelled above the wind at Bliss.

"He took a chance on it just like we're doing now. Slow up a minute at the first gas station after here, see if he got away with it or not." He knew that if he had, that meant they might just as well turn back then and there; Smiles was as good as dead already.

It didn't appear for another twenty minutes even at the

clip they had resumed once the bad stretch was past. With a flat, or until a tow car was sent out after anyone, it would have taken an hour or more to make it.

"Had a flat to fix, coming from our way, tonight?" Stillman yelled out at the attendant.

"And how!" the man yelled back, jogging over to them. "That was no flat! He wobbled up here with ribbons around his wheel. Rim all flattened, too, from riding so long on it."

"*He?*" echoed Stillman. "Wasn't there two women or anyway one, with him?"

"No, just a fellow alone."

"She probably waited for him up the road out of sight with Smiles," Bliss suggested in an undertone, "to avoid being seen; then he picked them up again when the job was finished. Or if Smiles was able to walk, maybe they detoured around it on foot and rejoined the car farther down."

"Heavy-set man with a bull neck, and little eyes, and scraggly red hair?" the constable asked the station operator.

"Yeah."

"That's him. How long ago did he pull out of here?"

"Not more than an hour ago, I'd say."

"See? We've already cut their head start plenty," Bliss rejoiced.

"There's still too damn much of it to suit me," was the detective's answer.

"One of you take the wheel for the next lap," Cochrane said. "The strain is telling on me. Better put these on for goggles." He handed Stillman his reading-glasses.

The filling-station and its circular glow of light whisked out behind them and they were on the tear once more. They picked up a State police motorcycle escort automatically within the next twenty minutes, by their mere speed in itself; simply tapered off long enough to show their badges and make their shouts of explanation heard. This was all to the good; it cleared their way through such towns and restricted-speed belts as lay in their path. Just to give an idea of their pace, there were times, on the straightaway, when their escort had difficulty in keeping up with them. And even so, they weren't making good enough time to satisfy Bliss. He alternated between fits of optimism, when he sat crouched forward on the edge of the seat, fists clenched, gritting: "We'll swing it; we'll get there in time; I know it!" and fits of despair, when he slumped back on his shoulder blades and groaned, "We'll never make it! I'm a fool; I should have let you phone in ahead like you wanted to! Can't you make this thing *move* at all?"

"Look at that speedometer," the man at the wheel suggested curtly. "There's nowhere else for the needle to go but off the dial altogether! Take it easy, Bliss. They can't possibly tear along at this clip; we're official, remember. Another thing, once they get there, they'll do a lot of cagey reconnoitering first. That'll eat up more of their head start. And finally, even after they get at it, they'll take it slow, make all their preparations first, to make it look right. Don't forget, they think they've got all night; they don't know we're on their trail."

"And it's still going to be an awful close shave," insisted Bliss through tightly clenched teeth.

Their State police escort signed off at the city limits with a wave of the arm, a hairpin turn, and left them on their own. They had to taper down necessarily now, even though traffic was light at this night hour. Bliss showed Stillman the shortcut over, which would bring them up to his house from the rear. A block and a half away Stillman choked off their engine, coasted to a stealthy stop under the overshadowing trees, and the long grueling race against time was over—without their knowing as yet whether it had been successful or not.

"Now follow me," Bliss murmured, hopping down. "I hope we didn't bring the car in too close; sounds carry so at an hour like this."

"They won't be expecting us." One of Stillman's legs gave under him from his long motionless stint at the wheel; he had to hobble along slapping at it until he could get the circulation back into it. Cochrane brought up at the rear.

When they cleared the back of the house next door to Bliss's and could look through the canal of separation to the street out in front, Bliss touched his companions on the arm, pointed meaningly. The blurred outline of a car was visible, parked there under the same leafy trees where Stillman himself had hidden when he was waiting for Bliss. They couldn't make out its interior.

"Someone in it," Cochrane said, breathing hard. "I think it's a woman, too. I can see the white curve of a bare arm on the wheel."

"You take that car, we'll take the house; he must be in there with her long ago at this stage of the game," Stillman muttered. "Can you come up on it quietly enough so she won't have time to sound the horn or signal him in any way?"

"I'll see to it I do!" was the purposeful answer. Cochrane turned back like a wraith, left the two of them alone.

They couldn't go near the front of the house because of the lookout, and there was no time to wait for Cochrane to incapacitate her. "Flatten out and do like I do," Bliss whispered. "She's probably watching the street out there more than this lot behind the house." He crouched, with his chin nearly down to his knees, darted across the intervening space to the concealment provided by the back of his own house.

"We can get in through the kitchen window," Bliss instructed, when Stillman had made the switch-over after him. "The latch never worked right. Give me a folder of matches, and make a footrest with your hands."

When he was up with one foot on the outside of the sill, his companion supporting the other, Bliss tore off and discarded the sandpaper and matches adhering to it, used the cardboard remainder as a sort of impromptu jimmy, slipping it down into the seam between the two window halves, and pushing the fastening back out of the way with it. A moment later he had the lower pane up and was inside the room, stretching down his hands to Stillman to help him up after him.

They both stood perfectly still there for a minute in the gloom, listening for all they were worth. Not a sound reached them, not a chink of light showed. Bliss felt a cold knife of doubt stab at his heart.

"Is he in here at all?" He breathed heavily. "That may be somebody else's car out there across the way."

At that instant there was the blurred but unmistakable sound that loose, falling earth makes, dropping back into a hollow or cavity. You hear it on the streets when a drainage ditch is being refilled. You hear it in a cemetery when a grave is being covered up. In the silence of this house, in the dead of night, it had a knell-like sound of finality. *Burial.*

Bliss gave a strangled gasp of horror, lurched forward in the darkness.

"He's already—through!"

The sound had seemed to come from somewhere underneath them. Bliss made for the basement door. Stillman's heavy footfalls pounded after him, all thought of concealment past.

Bliss clawed open the door that gave down to the cellar, flung it back. For a split second, and no more, dull-yellow light gleamed up from below. Then it snuffed out, too quickly to show them anything. There was pitch blackness below them, as above, and an ominous silence.

Something clicked just over Bliss's shoulder, and the pale moon of Stillman's torch glowed out from the cellar floor below them, started traveling around, looking for something to center on. Instantly a vicious tongue of flame spurted toward the parent orb, the reflector, and something flew past Bliss, went *spat* against the wall, as a thunderous boom sounded below.

Bliss could sense, rather than tell, that Stillman was raising his gun behind him. He clawed out, caught the cuff of the detective's sleeve, brought it down. "Don't! She may be down there somewhere in the line of fire!"

Something shot out over his shoulder. Not a gun or slug, but the torch itself. Stillman was trying to turn it into a sort of readymade star shell, by throwing it down there still lighted. The light pool on the floor streaked off like a comet, flicked across the ceiling, dropped down on the other side, and steadied itself against the far wall—with a pair of trouser legs caught squarely in the light, from the knees down. They buckled to jump aside, out of the revealing beam, but not quickly enough. Stillman sighted his gun at a kneecap and fired. The legs jolted, wobbled, folded up forward toward the light, bringing a torso and head down into view on the floor. When the fall ended, the beam of the torch was weirdly centered on the exact crown of a bald head surrounded by a circular fringe of reddish hair. It rolled from side to side like a giant ostrich egg, screaming agonizedly into the cellar floor.

"I'll take him," Stillman grunted. "You put on that light!"

Bliss groped for the dangling light cord that had proved such a hindrance to them just now by being down in the center of the basement instead of up by the doorway where they could get at it. He snagged it, found the finger switch, turned it. Horror flooded the place at his touch, in piebald tones of deep black shadow and pale yellow. The shovel Alden had just started to wield when he heard them coming lay half across a mound of freshly disinterred earth. Near it were the flat flagstones that had topped it, flooring the cellar, and the pickax that had loosened them. He must have brought the tools with him in the car, for they weren't Bliss's.

And on the other side of that mound—the short but deep hole the earth had come out of. Alden must have been working away down here for some time, to get so much done single-handed. And yet, though they had arrived before he'd finished, they were still too late—for in the hole, filling it to within an inch or two of the top, and fitting the sides even more closely, rested a deep old-fashioned trunk that had probably belonged to Smiles' mother and come down in the trunk compartment of the car. And four-square as it was, it looked ominously small for anyone to fit into—whole.

Bliss pointed down at it, moaned sickly. "She—she—"

He wanted to fold up and let himself topple inertly across the mound of earth before it. Stillman's sharp, whiplike command kept him upright. "Hang on! Coming!"

He had clipped the back of Alden's skull with his gun butt, to put him out of commission while their backs were turned. He leaped up on the mound of earth, and across the hole to the opposite side, then dropped down by the trunk, tugging at it.

"There's no blood around; he may have put her in alive. Hurry up, help me to get the lid up! Don't waste time trying to lift the whole thing out; just the lid. Get some air into it—"

It shot up between the two of them, and within lay a huddled bulk of sacking, pitifully doubled around on itself. *It was still moving feebly.* Fluttering spasmodically, rather than struggling any more.

The blade of the penknife Stillman had already used once before tonight flew out, slashed furiously at the coarse stuff. A contorted face was revealed through the rents, but not recognizable as Smiles' any more—a face black with suffocation, in which the last spark of life had been about to go out. And still might, if they didn't coax it back in a hurry.

They got her up out of it between them and straightened her out flat on the floor. Stillman sawed away at the short length of rope cruelly twisted around her neck, the cause of suffocation, severed it after seconds that seemed like centuries, unwound it, flung it off. Bliss, meanwhile, was stripping off the tattered remnants of the sacking. She was in a white silk slip.

Stillman straightened up, jumped for the stairs. "Breathe into her mouth like they do with choking kids. I'll send out a call for a Pulmotor."

But the battle was already won by the time he came

trooping down again; they could both tell that, laymen though they were. The congested darkness was leaving her face little by little, her chest was rising and falling of its own accord, she was coughing distressedly, and making little whimpering sounds of returning consciousness. They carried her up to the floor above when the emergency apparatus arrived, nevertheless, just to make doubly sure. It was while they were both up there, absorbed in watching the Pulmotor being used on her, that a single shot boomed out in the basement under them, with ominous finality.

Stillman clapped a hand to his hip. "Forgot to take his gun away from him. Well, there goes one of Cochrane's prisoners!"

They ran for the basement stairs, stopped halfway down them, one behind the other, looking at Alden's still form lying there below. It was still face-down, in the same position as before. One arm, curved under his own body at chest level, and a lazy tendril of smoke curling up around his ribs, told the difference.

"What a detective I am!" Stillman said disgustedly.

"It's better this way," Bliss answered, tight-lipped. "I think I would have killed him with my own bare hands, before they got him out of here, after what he tried to do to her tonight!"

By the time they returned upstairs again, Cochrane had come in with the woman. They were both being iodined and bandaged by an intern.

"What happened?" Stillman asked dryly. "Looks like she gave you more trouble than he gave us."

"Did you ever try to hang onto the outside of a wild car while the driver tried to shake you off? I'd gotten up to within one tree length of her, when the shots down in the basement tipped her off Alden was in for it. I just had time to make a flying tackle for the baggage rack before she was off a mile a minute. I had to work my way forward along the running-board, with her swerving and flinging around corners on two wheels. She finally piled up against a refuse-collection truck; dunno how it was we both weren't killed."

"Well, she's all yours, Cochrane," Stillman said. "But first I'm going to have to ask you to let me take her over to headquarters with me. You, too, Bliss." He looked at his watch. "I promised my lieutenant I'd be in with you by nine the latest, and I'm a stickler for keeping a promise. We'll be a little early, but unforeseen circumstances came up."

At headquarters, in the presence of Bliss, Stillman, Cochrane, the lieutenant of detectives, and the necessary police stenographer, Alden's accomplice was prevailed on to talk.

"My name is Irma Gilman," she began, "and I'm thirty-nine years old. I used to be a trained nurse on the staff of one of the large metropolitan hospitals. Two of my patients lost their lives through carelessness on my part, and I was discharged.

"I met Joe Alden six months ago. His wife was in ill health, so I moved in with them to look after her. Her first husband had left her well off, with slews of negotiable bonds. Alden had already helped himself to a few of them before I showed up, but now that I was there, he wanted to get rid of her altogether, so that we could get our hands on the rest. I told him he'd never get away with anything there, where everybody knew her; he'd have to take her somewhere else first. He went looking for a house, and when he'd found one that suited him, the place in Denby, he took me out to inspect it, without her, and palmed me off on the agent as his wife.

"We made all the arrangements, and when the day came to move, he went ahead with the moving van. I followed in the car with her after dark. That timed it so that we reached there late at night; there wasn't a soul around any more to see her go in. And from then on, as far as anyone in Denby knew, there were only two of us living in the house, not three. We didn't keep her locked up, but we put her in a bedroom at the back, where she couldn't be seen from the road, and put up a fine-meshed screen on the window. She was bed-ridden a good part of the time, anyway, and that made it easier to keep her presence concealed.

"He started to make his preparations from the moment we moved in. He began building this low wall out in front, as an excuse to order the bricks and other materials that he needed for the real work later on. He ordered more from the contractor than he needed, of course.

"Finally it happened. She felt a little better one day, came downstairs, and started checking over her list of bonds. He'd persuaded her when they were first married not to entrust them to a bank; she had them in an ordinary strongbox. She found out some of them were already missing. He went in there to her, and I listened outside the door. She didn't say very much, just: 'I thought I had more of these thousand-dollar bonds.' But that was enough to show us that she'd caught on. Then she got up very quietly and went out of the room without another word.

"Before we knew it, she was on the telephone in the hall—trying to get help, I suppose. She didn't have a chance to utter a word; he was too quick for her. He jumped out after her and pulled it away from her. He was between her and the front door, and she turned and went back upstairs, still without a sound, not even a scream. Maybe she still did not realize she was in bodily danger, thought she could get her things on and get out of the house.

"He said to me, 'Go outside and wait in front. Make sure there's no one anywhere in sight, up and down the road or in the fields.' I went out there, looked, raised my arm and dropped it, as a signal to him to go ahead. He went up the stairs after her.

"You couldn't hear a thing from inside. Not even a scream, or a chair falling over. He must have done it very quietly. In a while he came down to the door again. He was breathing a little fast and his face was a little pale, that was all. He said, 'It's over. I smothered her with one of the bed pillows. She didn't have much strength.' Then he went in again and carried her body down to the basement. We kept her down there while he went to work on this other wall; as

soon as it was up high enough, he put her behind it and finished it. He repainted the whole room so that one side
wouldn't look too new.

"Then, without a word of warning, the girl showed up
the other night. Luckily, just that night Joe had stayed down
at the hotel late having a few beers. He recognized her as
she got off the bus and brought her out with him in the car.
That did away with her having to ask her way of anyone. We
stalled her for a few minutes by pretending her mother was
fast asleep, until I had time to put a sedative in some tea I
gave her to drink. After that it was easy to handle her; we
put her down in the basement and kept her doped down
there.

"Joe remembered, from one of her letters, that she'd said
her husband had insured her, so that gave us our angle. The
next day I faked a long letter to her and mailed it to the city,
as if she'd never shown up here at all. Then when Bliss came
up looking for her, I tried to dope him, too, to give us a
chance to transport her back to his house during his absence, finish her off down there, and pin it on him. He
spoiled that by passing the food up and walking out on us.
The only thing left for us to do after that was for Joe to beat
the bus in, plant her clothes ahead of time, and put a bee in
the police's bonnet. That was just to get Bliss out of the
way, so the coast would be left clear to get her in down
there.

"We called his house from just inside the city limits when
we got down here with her tonight. No one answered, so it
seemed to have worked. But we'd lost a lot of time on account of that blowout. I waited outside in the car, with her
covered up on the floor, drugged. When Joe had the hole
dug, he came out and took her in with him.

"We thought all the risk we had to run was down at this
end. We were sure we were perfectly safe up at the other
end; Joe had done such a bang-up job on that wall. I still
can't understand how you caught onto it so quick."

"I'm an architect, that's why," Bliss said grimly. "There

was something about that room that bothered me. It wasn't on the square."

Smiles was lying in bed when Bliss went back to his own house, and she was pretty again. When she opened her eyes and looked up at him, they were all crinkly and smiling just as they used to be.

"Honey," she said, "it's so good to have you near me. I've learned my lesson. I'll never walk out on you again."

"That's right, you stay where you belong, with Ed," he said soothingly, "and nothing like that'll ever happen to you again."

MURDER ALWAYS
GATHERS MOMENTUM

Paine hung around outside the house waiting for old Ben Burroughs' caller to go, because he wanted to see him alone. You can't very well ask anyone for a loan of $250 in the presence of someone else, especially when you have a pretty strong hunch you're going to be turned down flat and told where to get off, into the bargain.

But he had a stronger reason for not wanting witnesses to his interview with the old skinflint. The large handkerchief in his back pocket, folded triangularly, had a special purpose, and that little instrument in another pocket—wasn't it to be used in prying open a window?

While he lurked in the shrubbery, watching the lighted window and Burroughs' seated form inside it, he kept rehearsing the plea he'd composed, as though he were still going to use it.

"Mr. Burroughs, I know it's late, and I know you'd rather not be reminded that I exist, but desperation can't wait; and I'm desperate." That sounded good. "Mr. Burroughs, I worked for your concern faithfully for ten long years, and the last six months of its existence, to help keep it going, I voluntarily worked at half-wages, on your given word that my defaulted pay would be made up as soon as things got better. Instead of that, you went into phony bankruptcy to cancel your obligations."

Then a little soft soap to take the sting out of it. "I haven't come near you all these years, and I haven't come to make trouble now. If I thought you really didn't have the money, I still wouldn't. But it's common knowledge by now that the bankruptcy was feigned; it's obvious by the way you continue to live that you salvaged your own investment; and

I've lately heard rumors of your backing a dummy corporation under another name to take up where you left off. Mr. Burroughs, the exact amount of the six months' promissory half-wages due me is two hundred and fifty dollars."

Just the right amount of dignity and self-respect, Pauline had commented at this point; not wishy-washy or maudlin, just quiet and effective.

And then for a bang-up finish, and every word of it true. "Mr. Burroughs, I have to have help tonight; it can't wait another twenty-four hours. There's a hole the size of a fifty-cent piece in the sole of each of my shoes; I have a wedge of cardboard in the bottom of each one. We haven't had light or gas in a week now. There's a bailiff coming tomorrow morning to put out the little that's left of our furniture and seal the door.

"If I was alone in this, I'd still fight it through, without going to anyone. But, Mr. Burroughs, I have a wife at home to support. You may not remember her, a pretty little dark-haired girl who once worked as a stenographer in your office for a month or two. You surely wouldn't know her now—she's aged twenty years in the past two."

That was about all. That was about all anyone could have said. And yet Paine knew he was licked before he even uttered a word of it.

He couldn't see the old man's visitor. The caller was out of range of the window. Burroughs was seated in a line with it, profile toward Paine. Paine could see his mean, thin-lipped mouth moving. Once or twice he raised his hand in a desultory gesture. Then he seemed to be listening and finally he nodded slowly. He held his forefinger up and shook it, as if impressing some point on his auditor. After that he rose and moved deeper into the room, but without getting out of line with the window.

He stood against the far wall, hand out to a tapestry hanging there. Paine craned his neck, strained his eyes. There must be a wall safe behind there the old codger was about to open.

If he only had a pair of binoculars handy.

Paine saw the old miser pause, turn his head and make some request of the other person. A hand abruptly grasped the looped shade cord and drew the shade to the bottom.

Paine gritted his teeth. The old fossil wasn't taking any chances, was he? You'd think he was a mind-reader, knew there was someone out there. But a chink remained, showing a line of light at the bottom. Paine sidled out of his hiding place and slipped up to the window. He put his eyes to it, focused on Burroughs' dialing hand, to the exclusion of everything else.

A three-quarters turn to the left, about to where the numeral 8 would be on the face of the clock. Then back to about where 3 would be. Then back the other way, this time to 10. Simple enough. He must remember that—8-3-10.

Burroughs was opening it now and bringing out a cashbox. He set it down on the table and opened it. Paine's eyes hardened and his mouth twisted sullenly. Look at all that money! The old fossil's gnarled hand dipped into it, brought out a sheaf of bills, counted them. He put back a few, counted the remainder a second time and set them on the tabletop while he returned the cashbox, closed the safe, straightened out the tapestry.

A blurred figure moved partly into the way at this point, too close to the shade gap to come clearly into focus; but without obliterating the little stack of bills on the table. Burroughs' claw-like hand picked them up, held them out. A second hand, smoother, reached for them. The two hands shook.

Paine prudently retreated to his former lookout point. He knew where the safe was now, that was all that mattered. He wasn't a moment too soon. The shade shot up an instant later, this time with Burroughs' hand guiding its cord. The other person had withdrawn offside again. Burroughs moved after him out of range, and the room abruptly darkened. A moment later a light flickered on in the porch ceiling.

Paine quickly shifted to the side of the house, in the moment's grace given him, in order to make sure his presence wasn't detected.

The door opened. Burroughs' voice croaked a curt "Night," to which the departing visitor made no answer. The interview had evidently not been an altogether cordial one. The door closed again, with quite a little force. A quick step crossed the porch, went along the cement walk to the street, away from where Paine stood pressed flat against the side of the house. He didn't bother trying to see who it was. It was too dark for that, and his primary purpose was to keep his own presence concealed.

When the anonymous tread had safely died away in the distance, Paine moved to where he could command the front of the house. Burroughs was alone in it now, he knew; he was too niggardly even to employ a full-time servant. A dim light showed for a moment or two through the fanlight over the door, coming from the back of the hall. Now was the time to ring the doorbell, if he expected to make his plea to the old duffer before he retired.

He knew that, and yet something seemed to be keeping him from stepping up onto the porch and ringing the doorbell. He knew what it was, too, but he wouldn't admit it to himself.

"He'll only say no point-blank and slam the door in my face" was the excuse he gave himself as he crouched back in the shrubbery, waiting. "And then once he's seen me out here, I'll be the first one he'll suspect afterwards when—"

The fanlight had gone dark now and Burroughs was on his way upstairs. A bedroom window on the floor above lighted up. There was still time; if he rang even now, Burroughs would come downstairs again and answer the door. But Paine didn't make the move, stayed there patiently waiting.

The bedroom window blacked out at last, and the house was now dark and lifeless. Paine stayed there, still fighting with himself. Not a battle, really, because that had been lost

long ago; but still giving himself excuses for what he kne
he was about to do. Excuses for not going off about h
business and remaining what he had been until now—a
honest man.

How could he face his wife, if he came back empt
handed tonight? Tomorrow their furniture would be pil
on the sidewalk. Night after night he had promised to tack
Burroughs, and each time he'd put it off, walked past th
house without summoning up nerve enough to go throug
with it. Why? For one thing, he didn't have the courage t
stomach the sharp-tongued, sneering refusal that he wa
sure he'd get. But the more important thing had been th
realization that once he made his plea, he automatically ca
celed this other, unlawful way of getting the money. Bu
roughs had probably forgotten his existence after all thes
years, but if he reminded him of it by interviewing hi
ahead of time—

He tightened his belt decisively. Well, he wasn't comir
home to her empty-handed tonight, but he still wasn't goir
to tackle Burroughs for it either. She'd never need to fin
out just how he'd got it.

He straightened and looked all around him. No one i
sight. The house was isolated. Most of the streets around
were only laid out and paved by courtesy; they border
vacant lots. He moved in cautiously but determinedly to
ward the window of that room where he had seen the safe.

Cowardice can result in the taking of more risks than th
most reckless courage. He was afraid of little things—afrai
of going home and facing his wife empty-handed, afraid
asking an ill-tempered old reprobate for money because h
knew he would be reviled and driven away—and so he wa
about to break into a house, become a burglar for the fir:
time in his life.

It opened so easily. It was almost an invitation to unlaw
ful entry. He stood up on the sill, and the cover of a pape
book of matches, thrust into the intersection between th
two window halves, pushed the tongue of the latch out c

the way.

He dropped down to the ground, applied the little instrument he had brought to the lower frame, and it slid effortlessly up. A minute later he was in the room, had closed the window so it wouldn't look suspicious from the outside. He wondered why he'd always thought until now it took skill and patience to break into a house. There was nothing to it.

He took out the folded handkerchief and tied it around the lower part of his face. For a minute he wasn't going to bother with it, and later he was sorry he had, in one way. And then again, it probably would have happened anyway, even without it. It wouldn't keep him from being seen, only from being identified.

He knew enough not to light the room lights, but he had nothing so scientific as a pocket torch with him to take their place. He had to rely on ordinary matches, which meant he could only use one hand for the safe dial, after he had cleared the tapestry out of the way.

It was a toy thing, a gimcrack. He hadn't even the exact combination, just the approximate position—8-3-10. It wouldn't work the first time, so he varied it slightly, and then it clicked free.

He opened it, brought out the cashbox, set it on the table. It was as though the act of setting it down threw a master electric switch. The room was suddenly drenched with light and Burroughs stood in the open doorway, bathrobe around his weazened frame, left hand out to the wall switch, right hand holding a gun trained on Paine.

Paine's knees knocked together, his windpipe constricted, and he died a little—the way only an amateur caught redhanded at his first attempt can, a professional never. His thumb stung unexpectedly, and he mechanically whipped out the live match he was holding.

"Just got down in time, didn't I?" the old man said with spiteful satisfaction. "It mayn't be much of a safe, but it sets off a buzzer up by my bed every time it swings open—see?"

He should have moved straight across to the phone, right there in the room with Paine, and called for help, but he had a vindictive streak in him; he couldn't resist standing and rubbing it in.

"Ye know what ye're going to get for this, don't ye?" he went on, licking his indrawn lips. "And I'll see that ye get it too, every last month of it that's coming to ye." He took a step forward. "Now get away from that. Get all the way back over there and don't ye make a move until I—"

A sudden dawning suspicion entered his glittering little eyes. "Wait a minute. Haven't I seen you somewhere before? There's something familiar about you." He moved closer. "Take off that mask," he ordered. "Let me see who the devil you are!"

Paine became panic-stricken at the thought of revealing his face. He didn't stop to think that as long as Burroughs had him at gunpoint anyway, and he couldn't get away, the old man was bound to find out who he was sooner or later.

He shook his head in unreasoning terror.

"No!" he panted hoarsely, billowing out the handkerchief over his mouth. He even tried to back away, but there was a chair or something in the way, and he couldn't.

That brought the old man in closer. "Then by golly I'll take it off for ye!" he snapped. He reached out for the lower triangular point of it. His right hand slanted out of line with Paine's body as he did so, was no longer exactly covering it with the gun. But the variation was nothing to take a chance on.

Cowardice. Cowardice that spurs you to a rashness the stoutest courage would quail from. Paine didn't stop to think of the gun. He suddenly hooked onto both the old man's arms, spread-eagled them. It was such a harebrained chance to take that Burroughs wasn't expecting it, and accordingly it worked. The gun clicked futilely, pointed up toward the ceiling; it must have jammed, or else the first chamber was empty and Burroughs hadn't known it.

Paine kept warding that arm off at a wide angle. But his

chief concern was the empty hand clawing toward the handkerchief. That he swiveled far downward the other way, out
of reach. He twisted the scrawny skin around the old man's
skinny right wrist until pain made the hand flop over open
and drop the gun. It fell between them to the floor, and
Paine scuffed it a foot or two out of reach with the side of
his foot.

Then he locked that same foot behind one of Burroughs'
and pushed him over it. The old man went sprawling backwards on the floor, and the short, unequal struggle was over.
Yet even as he went, he was victorious. His down-flung left
arm, as Paine released it to send him over, swept up in an
arc, clawed, and took the handkerchief with it.

He sprawled there now, cradled on the point of one elbow, breathing malign recognition that was like a knife
through Paine's heart. "You're Dick Paine, you dirty crook!
I know ye now! You're Dick Paine, my old employee!
You're going to pay for this—"

That was all he had time to say. That was his own death
warrant. Paine was acting under such neuromuscular com-
pulsion, brought on by the instinct of self-preservation, that
he wasn't even conscious of stooping to retrieve the fallen
gun. The next thing he knew it was in his hand, pointed toward the accusing mouth, which was all he was afraid of.

He jerked the trigger. For the second time it clicked—
either jammed or unloaded at that chamber. He was to have
that on his conscience afterwards, that click—like a last
chance given him to keep from doing what he was about to
do. That made it something different, that took away the
shadowy little excuse he would have had until now; that
changed it from an impulsive act committed in the heat of
combat to a deed of cold-blooded, deliberate murder, with
plenty of time to think twice before it was committed. And
conscience makes cowards of us all. And he was a coward to
begin with.

Burroughs even had time to sputter the opening syllables
of a desperate plea for mercy, a promise of immunity. True,

he probably wouldn't have kept it.

"Don't! Paine—Dick, don't! I won't say anything. I won't tell 'em you were here—"

But Burroughs knew who he was. Paine tugged at the trigger, and the third chamber held death in it. This time the gun crashed, and Burroughs' whole face was veiled in a huff of smoke. By the time it had thinned he was already dead, head on the floor, a tenuous thread of red streaking from the corner of his mouth, as though he had no more than split his lip.

Paine was the amateur even to the bitter end. In the death hush that followed, his first half-audible remark was: "Mr. Burroughs, I didn't mean to—"

Then he just stared in white-faced consternation. "Now I've done it! I've killed a man—and they kill you for that! Now I'm in for it!"

He looked at the gun, appalled, as though it alone, and not he, was to blame for what had happened. He picked up the handkerchief, dazedly rubbed at the weapon, then desisted again. It seemed to him safer to take it with him, even though it was Burroughs' own. He had an amateur's mystic dread of fingerprints. He was sure he wouldn't be able to clean it thoroughly enough to remove all traces of his own handling; even in the very act of trying to clean it, he might leave others. He sheathed it in the inner pocket of his coat.

He looked this way and that. He'd better get out of here; he'd better get out of here. Already the drums of flight were beginning to beat in him, and he knew they'd never be silent again.

The cashbox was still standing there on the table where he'd left it, and he went to it, flung the lid up. He didn't want this money any more; it had curdled for him; it had become bloody money. But he had to have some, at least, to make it easier to keep from getting caught. He didn't stop to count how much there was in it; there must have been at least a thousand, by the looks of it. Maybe even fifteen or eighteen hundred.

He wouldn't take a cent more than was coming to him.

He'd only take the two hundred and fifty he'd come here to get. To his frightened mind that seemed to make his crime less heinous, if he contented himself with taking just what was rightfully his. That seemed to keep it from being outright murder and robbery, enabled him to maintain the fiction that it had been just a collection of a debt accompanied by a frightful and unforeseen accident. And one's conscience, after all, is the most dreaded policeman of the lot.

And furthermore, he realized as he hastily counted it out, thrust the sum into his back trouser pocket, buttoned the pocket down, he couldn't tell his wife that he'd been here— or she'd know what he'd done. He'd have to make her think that he'd got the money somewhere else. That shouldn't be hard. He'd put off coming here to see Burroughs night after night; he'd shown her plainly that he hadn't relished the idea of approaching his former boss. She'd been the one who had kept egging him on.

Only tonight she'd said, "I don't think you'll ever carry it out. I've about given up hope."

So what more natural than to let her think that in the end he hadn't? He'd think up some other explanation to account for the presence of the money; he'd have to. If not right tonight, then tomorrow. It would come to him after the shock of this had worn off a little and he could think more calmly.

Had he left anything around that would betray him, that they could trace to him? He'd better put the cashbox back; there was just a chance that they wouldn't know exactly how much the old skinflint had had on hand. They often didn't, with his type. He wiped it off carefully with the handkerchief he'd had around his face, twisted the dial closed on it, dabbed at that. He didn't go near the window again; he put out the light and made his way out by the front door of the house.

He opened it with the handkerchief and closed it after him again, and after an exhaustive survey of the desolate

street, came down off the porch, moved quickly along the
front walk, turned left along the gray tape of sidewalk that
threaded the gloom, toward the distant trolley line that he
wasn't going to board at this particular stop, at this particular hour.

He looked up once or twice at the star-flecked sky as he
trudged along. It was over. That was all there was to it. Just
a jealously guarded secret now. A memory that he daren't
share with anyone else, not even Pauline. But deep within
him he knew better. It wasn't over, it was just beginning.
That had been just the curtain raiser, back there. Murder,
like a snowball rolling down a slope, gathers momentum as
it goes.

He had to have a drink. He had to try to drown the damn
thing out of him. He couldn't go home dry with it on his
mind. They stayed open until four, didn't they, places like
that? He wasn't much of a drinker; he wasn't familiar with
details like that. Yes, there was one over there, on the other
side of the street. And this was far enough away, more than
two-thirds of the way from Burroughs' to his own place.

It was empty. That might be better; then again it might
not. He could be too easily remembered. Well, too late now,
he was already at the bar. "A straight whiskey." The barman
didn't even have time to turn away before he spoke again.
"Another one."

He shouldn't have done that; that looked suspicious, to
gulp it that quick.

"Turn that radio off," he said hurriedly. He shouldn't
have said that; that sounded suspicious. The barman had
looked at him when he did. And the silence was worse, if
anything. Unbearable. Those throbbing drums of danger.
"Never mind, turn it on again."

"Make up your mind, mister," the barman said in mild
reproof.

He seemed to be doing all the wrong things. He shouldn't
have come in here at all, to begin with. Well, he'd get out,
before he put his foot in it any worse. "How much?" He

took out the half-dollar and the quarter that was all he had.

"Eighty cents."

His stomach dropped an inch. Not *that* money! He didn't want to have to bring that out, it would show too plainly on his face. "Most places, they charge thirty-five a drink."

"Not this brand. You didn't specify." But the barman was on guard now, scenting a deadbeat. He was leaning over the counter, right square in front of him, in a position to take in every move he made with his hands.

He shouldn't have ordered that second drink. Just for a nickel he was going to have to take that whole wad out right under this man's eyes. And maybe he would remember that tomorrow, after the jumpy way Paine had acted in here!

"Where's the washroom?"

"That door right back there behind the cigarette machine." But the barman was now plainly suspicious; Paine could tell that by the way he kept looking at him.

Paine closed it after him, sealed it with his shoulder-blades, unbuttoned his back pocket, riffled through the money, looking for the smallest possible denomination. A ten was the smallest, and there was only one of them; that would have to do. He cursed himself for getting into such a spot.

The door suddenly gave a heave behind him. Not a violent one, but he wasn't expecting it. It threw him forward off balance. The imperfectly grasped outspread fan of money in his hand went scattering all over the floor. The barman's head showed through the aperture. He started to say: "I don't like the way you're acting. Come on now, get out of my pla—" Then he saw the money.

Burroughs' gun had been an awkward bulk for his inside coat pocket all along. The grip was too big; it overspanned the lining. His abrupt lurch forward had shifted it. It felt as if it was about to fall out of its own weight. He clutched at it to keep it in.

The barman saw the gesture, closed in on him with a grunted "I thought so!" that might have meant nothing or everything.

He was no Burroughs to handle; he was an ox of a man. He pinned Paine back against the wall and held him there more or less helpless. Even so, if he'd only shut up, it probably wouldn't have happened. But he made a tunnel of his mouth and bayed: "Pol-eece! Holdup! Help!"

Paine lost the little presence of mind he had left, became a blurred pinwheel of hand motion, impossible to control or forestall. Something exploded against the barman's midriff, as though he'd had a firecracker tucked in under his belt.

He coughed his way down to the floor and out of the world.

Another one. Two now. Two in less than an hour. Paine didn't think the words; they seemed to glow out at him, emblazoned on the grimy washroom walls in characters of fire, like in that biblical story.

He took a step across the prone, white-aproned form as stiffly as though he were high up on stilts. He looked out through the door crack. No one in the bar. And it probably hadn't been heard outside in the street; it had had two doors to go through.

He put the damned thing away, the thing that seemed to be spreading death around just by being in his possession. If he hadn't brought it with him from Burroughs' house, this man would have been alive now. But if he hadn't brought it with him, he would have been apprehended for the first murder by now. Why blame the weapon, why not just blame fate?

That money, all over the floor. He squatted, went for it bill by bill, counting it as he went. Twenty, forty, sixty, eighty. Some of them were on one side of the corpse, some on the other; he had to cross over, not once but several times, in the course of his grisly paper chase. One was even pinned partly under him, and when he'd wangled it out, there was a swirl of blood on the edge. He grimaced, thrust it out, blotted it off. Some of it stayed on, of course.

He had it all now, or thought he did. He couldn't stay in

here another minute; he felt as if he were choking. He got it all into his pocket any old way, buttoned it down. Then he eased out, this time looking behind him at what he'd done, not before him. That was how he missed seeing the drunk, until it was too late and the drunk had already seen him.

The drunk was pretty drunk, but maybe not drunk enough to take a chance on. He must have weaved in quietly, while Paine was absorbed in retrieving the money. He was bending over reading the list of selections on the coin phonograph. He raised his head before Paine could get back in again, and to keep him from seeing what lay on the floor in there Paine quickly closed the door behind him.

"Say, itsh about time," the drunk complained. "How about a little servish here?"

Paine tried to shadow his face as much as he could with the brim of his hat. "I'm not in charge here," he mumbled, "I'm just a customer myself—"

The drunk was going to be sticky. He barnacled onto Paine's lapels as he tried to sidle by. "Don't gimme that. You just hung up your coat in there; you think you're quitting for the night. Well, you ain't quitting until I've had my drink—"

Paine tried to shake him off without being too violent about it and bringing on another hand-to-hand set-to. He hung on like grim death. Or rather, he hung on to grim death—without knowing it.

Paine fought down the flux of panic, the ultimate result of which he'd already seen twice now. Any minute someone might come in from the street. Someone sober. "All right," he breathed heavily, "hurry up, what'll it be?"

"Thass more like it; now you're being reg'lar guy." The drunk released him and he went around behind the bar. "Never anything but good ole Four Roses for mine truly—"

Paine snatched down a bottle at random from the shelf, handed it over bodily. "Here, help yourself. You'll have to take it outside with you, I'm—we're closing up for the night now." He found a switch, threw it. It only made part of the lights go out. There was no time to bother with the rest. He hustled the bottle-nursing drunk out ahead of him, pulled the door to after the two of them, so that it would appear to be locked even if it wasn't.

The drunk started to make a loud plaint, looping around on the sidewalk. "You're a fine guy, not even a glass to drink it out of!"

Paine gave him a slight push in one direction, wheeled and made off in the other.

The thing was, how drunk was he? Would he remember Paine; would he know him if he saw him again? He hurried on, spurred to a run by the night-filling hails and imprecations resounding behind him. He couldn't do it again. Three lives in an hour. He couldn't!

The night was fading when he turned into the little courtyard that was his own. He staggered up the stairs, but not from the two drinks he'd had, from the two deaths.

He stood outside his own door at last—3-B. It seemed such a funny thing to do after killing people—fumble around in your pockets for your latchkey and fit it in, just like other nights. He'd been an honest man when he'd left here, and now he'd come back a murderer. A double one.

He hoped she was asleep. He couldn't face her right now, couldn't talk to her even if he tried. He was all in emotionally. She'd find out right away just by looking at his face, by looking in his eyes.

He eased the front door closed, tiptoed to the bedroom, looked in. She was lying there asleep. Poor thing, poor helpless thing, married to a murderer.

He went back, undressed in the outer room. Then he stayed in there. Not even stretched out on top of the sofa, but crouched beside it on the floor, head and arms pillowed against its seat. The drums of terror kept pounding. They kept saying, "What am I gonna do now?"

The sun seemed to shoot up in the sky, it got to the top

so fast. He opened his eyes and it was all the way up. He went to the door and brought in the paper. It wasn't in the morning papers yet; they were made up too soon after midnight.

He turned around and Pauline had come out, was picking up his things. "All over the floor, never saw a man like you—"

He said, "Don't—" and stabbed his hand toward her, but it was already too late. He'd jammed the bills in so haphazardly the second time, in the bar, that they made a noticeable bulge there in his back pocket. She opened it and took them out, and some of them dribbled onto the floor.

She just stared. "Dick!" She was incredulous, overjoyed. "Not Burroughs? Don't tell me you finally—"

"No!" The name went through him like a red-hot skewer. "I didn't go anywhere near him. He had nothing to do with it!"

She nodded corroboratively. "I thought not, because—"

He wouldn't let her finish. He stepped close to her, took her by both shoulders. "Don't mention his name to me again. I don't want to hear his name again. I got it from someone else."

"Who?"

He knew he'd have to answer her, or she'd suspect something. He swallowed, groped blindly for a name. "Charlie Chalmers," he blurted out.

"But he refused you only last week!"

"Well, he changed his mind." He turned on her tormentedly. "Don't ask me any more questions, Pauline; I can't stand it! I haven't slept all night. There it is; that's all that matters." He took his trousers from her, went into the bathroom to dress. He'd hidden Burroughs' gun the night before in the built-in laundry hamper in there; he wished he'd hidden the money with it. He put the gun back in the pocket where he'd carried it last night. If she touched him there—

He combed his hair. The drums were a little quieter now, but he knew they'd come back again; this was just the lull before the storm.

He came out again, and she was putting cups on the table. She looked worried now. She sensed that something was wrong. She was afraid to ask him, he could see, maybe afraid of what she'd find out. He couldn't sit here eating, just as though this was any other day. Any minute someone might come here after him.

He passed by the window. Suddenly he stiffened, gripped the curtain. "What's that man doing down there?" She came up behind him. "Standing there talking to the janitor—"

"Why, Dick, what harm is there in that? A dozen people a day stop and chat with—"

He edged back a step behind the frame. "He's looking up at our windows! Did you see that? They both turned and looked up this way! Get back!" His arm swept her around behind him.

"Why should we? We haven't done anything."

"They're coming in the entrance to this wing! They're on their way up here—"

"Dick, why are you acting this way, what's happened?"

"Go in the bedroom and wait there." He was a coward, yes. But there are varieties. At least he wasn't a coward that hid behind a woman's skirts. He prodded her in there ahead of him. Then he gripped her shoulder a minute. "Don't ask any questions. If you love me, stay in here until they go away again."

He closed the door on her frightened face. He cracked the gun. Two left in it. "I can get them both," he thought, "if I'm careful. I've got to."

It was going to happen again.

The jangle of the doorbell battery steeled him. He moved with deadly slowness toward the door, feet flat and firm upon the floor. He picked up the newspaper from the table on his way by, rolled it into a funnel, thrust his hand and the gun down into it. The pressure of his arm against his side was sufficient to keep it furled. It was as though he had just been reading and had carelessly tucked the paper under his arm. It hid the gun effectively as long as he kept it slanting down.

He freed the latch and shifted slowly back with the door, bisected by its edge, the unarmed half of him all that showed. The janitor came into view first, as the gap widened. He was on the outside. The man next to him had a derby hat riding the back of his head, a bristly mustache, was rotating a cigar between his teeth. He looked like—one of those who come after you.

The janitor said with scarcely veiled insolence, "Paine, I've got a man here looking for a flat. I'm going to show him yours, seeing as how it'll be available from today on. Any objections?"

Paine swayed there limply against the door like a garment bag hanging on a hook, as they brushed by. "No," he whispered deflatedly. "No, go right ahead."

He held the door open to make sure their descent continued all the way down to the bottom. As soon as he'd closed it, Pauline caught him anxiously by the arm. "Why wouldn't you let me tell them we're able to pay the arrears now and are staying? Why did you squeeze my arm like that?"

"Because we're not staying, and I don't want them to know we've got the money. I don't want anyone to know. We're getting out of here."

"Dick, what is it? Have you done something you shouldn't?"

"Don't ask me. Listen, if you love me, don't ask any questions. I'm—in a little trouble. I've got to get out of here. Never mind why. If you don't want to come with me, I'll go alone."

"Anywhere you go, I'll go." Her eyes misted. "But can't it be straightened out?"

Two men dead beyond recall. He gave a bitter smile. "No, it can't."

"Is it bad?"

He shut his eyes, took a minute to answer. "It's bad, Pauline. That's all you need to know. That's all I want you to know. I've got to get out of here as fast as I can. From one minute to the next it may be too late. Let's get started now. They'll be here to dispossess us sometime today anyway; that'll be a good excuse. We won't wait, we'll leave now."

She went in to get ready. She took so long doing it he nearly went crazy. She didn't seem to realize how urgent it was. She wasted as much time deciding what to take and what to leave behind as though they were going on a weekend jaunt to the country. He kept going to the bedroom door, urging, "Pauline, hurry! Faster, Pauline!"

She cried a great deal. She was an obedient wife; she didn't ask him any more questions about what the trouble was. She just cried about it without knowing what it was.

He was down on hands and knees beside the window, in the position of a man looking for a collar button under a dresser, when she finally came out with the small bag she'd packed. He turned a stricken face to her. "Too late—I can't leave with you. Someone's already watching the place."

She inclined herself to his level, edged up beside him.

"Look straight over to the other side of the street. See him? He hasn't moved for the past ten minutes. People don't just stand like that for no reason—"

"He may be waiting for someone."

"He is," he murmured somberly. "Me."

"But you can't be sure."

"No, but if I put it to the test by showing myself, it'll be too late by the time I find out. You go by yourself, ahead of me."

"No, if you stay, let me stay with you—"

"I'm not staying; I can't! I'll follow you and meet you somewhere. But it'll be easier for us to leave one at a time than both together. I can slip over the roof or go out the basement way. He won't stop you; they're not looking for you. You go now and wait for me. No, I have a better idea.

Here's what you do. You get two tickets and get on the train at the downtown terminal without waiting for me——" He was separating some of the money, thrusting it into her reluctant hand while he spoke. "Now listen closely. Two tickets to Montreal——"

An added flicker of dismay showed in her eyes. "We're leaving the country?"

When you've committed murder, you have no country any more. "We have to, Pauline. Now, there's an eight o'clock limited for there every night. It leaves the downtown terminal at eight sharp. It stops for five minutes at the station uptown at twenty after. That's where I'll get on. Make sure you're on it or we'll miss each other. Keep a seat for me next to you in the day coach——"

She clung to him despairingly. "No, no. I'm afraid you won't come. Something'll happen. You'll miss it. If I leave you now I may never see you again. I'll find myself making the trip up there alone, without you——"

He tried to reassure her, pressing her hands between his. "Pauline, I give you my word of honor——" That was no good, he was a murderer now. "Pauline, I swear to you——"

"Here——on this. Take a solemn oath on this, otherwise I won't go." She took out a small carnelian cross she carried in her handbag, attached to a little gold chain——one of the few things they hadn't pawned. She palmed it, pressed the flat of his right hand over it. They looked into each other's eyes with sacramental intensity.

His voice trembled. "I swear nothing will keep me from that train; I'll join you on it no matter what happens, no matter who tries to stop me. Rain or shine, *dead or alive,* I'll meet you aboard it at eight-twenty tonight!"

She put it away, their lips brushed briefly but fervently.

"Hurry up now," he urged. "He's still there. Don't look at him on your way past. If he should stop you and ask who you are, give another name——"

He went to the outside door with her, watched her start down the stairs. The last thing she whispered up was: "Dick, be careful for my sake. Don't let anything happen to you between now and tonight."

He went back to the window, crouched down, cheek-bones to sill. She came out under him in a minute or two. She knew enough not to look up at their windows, although the impulse must have been strong. The man was still standing over there. He didn't seem to notice her. He even looked off in another direction.

She passed from view behind the building line; their windows were set in on the court that indented it. Paine wondered if he'd ever see her again. Sure he would; he had to. He realized that it would be better for her if he didn't. It wasn't fair to enmesh her in his own doom. But he'd sworn an oath, and he meant to keep it.

Two, three minutes ticked by. The cat-and-mouse play continued. He crouched motionless by the window; the other man stood motionless across the street. She must be all the way down at the corner by now. She'd take the bus there, to go downtown. She might have to wait a few minutes for one to come along; she might still be in sight. But if the man was going to go after her, accost her, he would have started by now. He wouldn't keep standing there.

Then, as Paine watched, he did start. He looked down that way, threw away something he'd been smoking, began to move purposefully in that direction. There was no mistaking the fact that he was looking *at* or *after* someone, by the intent way he held his head. He passed from sight.

Paine began to breathe hot and fast. "I'll kill him. If he touches her, tries to stop her, I'll kill him right out in the open street in broad daylight." It was still fear, cowardice, that was at work, although it was almost unrecognizable as such by now.

He felt for the gun, left his hand on it, inside the breast of his coat, straightened to his feet, ran out of the flat and down the stairs. He cut across the little set-in paved court-yard at a sprint, flashed out past the sheltering building line, turned down in the direction they had both taken.

Then as the panorama before him registered, he staggered to an abrupt stop, stood taking it in. It offered three component but separate points of interest. He only noticed two at first. One was the bus down at the corner. The front-third of it protruded, door open. He caught a glimpse of Pauline's back as she was in the act of stepping in, unaccompanied and unmolested.

The door closed automatically, and it swept across the vista and disappeared at the other side. On the other side of the street, but nearer at hand, the man who had been keeping the long vigil had stopped a second time, was gesticulating angrily to a woman laden with parcels whom he had joined. Both voices were so raised they reached Paine without any trouble.

"A solid half-hour I've been standing there and no one home to let me in!"

"Well, is it my fault you went off without your key? Next time take it with you!"

Nearer at hand still, on Paine's own side of the street, a lounging figure detached itself from the building wall and impinged on his line of vision. The man had been only yards away the whole time, but Paine's eyes had been trained on the distance; he'd failed to notice him until now.

His face suddenly loomed out at Paine. His eyes bored into Paine's with unmistakable intent. He didn't look like one of those that come to get you. He acted like it. He thumbed his vest pocket for something, some credential or identification. He said in a soft, slurring voice that held an inflexible command in it, "Just a minute there, buddy. Your name's Paine, ain't it? I want to see you—"

Paine didn't have to give his muscular coordination any signal; it acted for him automatically. He felt his legs carry him back into the shelter of the courtyard in a sort of slithering jump. He was in at the foot of the public stairs before the other man had even rounded the building line. He was in behind his own door before the remorselessly slow but plainly audible tread had started up them.

The man seemed to be coming up after him alone. Didn't he know Paine had a gun? He'd find out. He was up on the landing now. He seemed to know which floor to stop at, which door to come to a halt before. Probably the janitor had told him. Then why hadn't he come sooner? Maybe he'd been waiting for someone to join him, and Paine had upset the plan by showing himself so soon.

Paine realized he'd trapped himself by returning here. He should have gone on up to the roof and over. But the natural instinct of the hunted, whether four-legged or two, is to find a hole, get in out of the open. It was too late now: he was right out there on the other side of the door. Paine tried to keep his harried breathing silent.

To his own ears it grated like sand sifted through a sieve.

He didn't ring the bell and he didn't knock; he tried the knob, in a half-furtive, half-badgering way. That swirl of panic began to churn in Paine again. He couldn't let him get in; he couldn't let him get away, either. He'd only go and bring others back with him.

Paine pointed the muzzle of the gun to the crack of the door, midway between the two hinges. With his other hand he reached out for the catch that controlled the latch, released it.

Now, if he wanted to die, he should open this door. The man had kept on trying the knob. Now the door slipped in past the frame. The crack at the other side widened in accompaniment as it swung around. Paine ran the gun bore up it even with the side of his head.

The crash was thunderous. He fell into the flat, with only his feet and ankles outside.

Paine came out from behind the door, dragged him the rest of the way in, closed it. He stopped, his hands probed here and there. He found a gun, a heftier, more businesslike one than his. He took that. He found a billfold heavy with cash. He took that, too. He fished for the badge.

There wasn't any in the vest pocket he'd seen him reach toward downstairs. There was only a block of cheaply printed cards. *Star Finance Company. Loans. Up to any amount without security.*

So he hadn't been one, after all; he'd evidently been some kind of a loan shark, drawn by the scent of Paine's difficulties.

Three times now in less than twenty-four hours.

Instinctively he knew he was doomed now, if he hadn't before. There wasn't any more of the consternation he had felt the first two times. He kept buying off time with bullets; that was all it was now. And the rate of interest kept going higher; the time limit kept shortening. There wasn't even any time to feel sorry.

Doors had begun opening outside in the hall; voices were calling back and forth. "What was that—a shot?"

"It sounded like in 3-B."

He'd have to get out now, right away, or he'd be trapped in here again. And this time for good. He shifted the body out of the line of vision from outside, buttoned up his jacket, took a deep breath; then he opened the door, stepped out, closed it after him. Each of the other doors was open with someone peering out from it. They hadn't ganged up yet in the middle of the hall. Most of them were women, anyway. One or two edged timidly back when they saw him emerge.

"It wasn't anything," he said. "I dropped a big clay jug in there just now."

He knew they didn't believe him.

He started down the stairs. At the third step he looked over the side, saw the cop coming up. Somebody had already phoned or sent out word. He reversed, flashed around his own landing, and on up from there.

The cop's voice said, "Stop where you are!" He was coming on fast now. But Paine was going just as fast.

The cop's voice said, "Get inside, all of you! I'm going to shoot!"

Doors began slapping shut like firecrackers. Paine switched over abruptly to the rail and shot first.

The cop jolted, but he grabbed the rail and stayed up. He didn't die as easy as the others. He fired four times before he lost his gun. He missed three times and hit Paine the fourth time.

It went in his chest on the right side, and knocked him across the width of the staircase. It flamed with pain, and then it didn't hurt so much. He found he could get up again. Maybe because he had to. He went back and looked down. The cop had folded over the railing and gone sliding down it as far as the next turn, the way a kid does on a banister. Only sidewise, on his stomach. Then he dropped off onto the landing, rolled over and lay still, looking up at Paine without seeing him.

Four.

Paine went on up to the roof, but not fast, not easily any more. The steps were like an escalator going the other way, trying to carry him down with them. He went across to the roof of the next flat, and down through that, and came out on the street behind his own. The two buildings were twins, set back to back. The prowl car was already screeching to a stop, out of sight back there at his own doorway. He could hear it over the roofs, on this side.

He was wet across the hip. Then he was wet as far down as the knee. And he hadn't been hit in those places, so he must be bleeding a lot. He saw a taxi and he waved to it, and it backed up and got him. It hurt getting in. He couldn't answer for a minute when the driver asked him where to. His sock felt sticky under his shoe now, from the blood. He wished he could stop it until eight-twenty. He had to meet Pauline on the train, and that was a long time to stay alive.

The driver had taken him off the street and around the corner without waiting for him to be more explicit. He asked where to, a second time.

Paine said, "What time is it?"

"Quarter to six, cap."

Life was awfully short—and awfully sweet. He said,

"Take me to the park and drive me around in it." That was the safest thing to do, that was the only place they wouldn't look for you.

He thought, "I've always wanted to drive around in the park. Not go anywhere, just drive around in it slow. I never had the money to do it before."

He had it now. More money than he had time left to spend it.

The bullet must still be in him. His back didn't hurt, so it hadn't come out. Something must have stopped it. The bleeding had let up. He could feel it drying on him. The pain kept trying to pull him over double though.

The driver noticed it, said: "Are you hurt?"

"No, I've got kind of a cramp, that's all."

"Want me to take you to a drug store?"

Paine smiled weakly. "No, I guess I'll let it ride."

Sundown in the park. So peaceful, so prosaic. Long shadows across the winding paths. A belated nursemaid or two pushing a perambulator homeward. A loiterer or two lingering on the benches in the dusk. A little lake, with a rowboat on it—a sailor on shore leave rowing his sweetheart around. A lemonade and popcorn man trundling his wagon home for the day.

Stars were coming out. At times the trees were outlined black against the copper western sky. At times the whole thing blurred and he felt as if he were being carried around in a maelstrom. Each time he fought through and cleared his senses again. He had to make that train.

"Let me know when it gets to be eight o'clock."

"Sure, cap. It's only quarter to seven now."

A groan was torn from Paine as they hit a lumpy spot in the driveway. He tried to keep it low, but the driver must have heard it.

"Still hurts you, huh?" he inquired sympathetically. "You oughta get it fixed up." He began to talk about his own indigestion. "Take me, for instance. I'm okay until I eat tamales and root beer. Any time that I eat tamales and root beer—"

He shut up abruptly. He was staring fixedly into the rear-sight mirror. Paine warily clutched his lapels together over his darkened shirt front. He knew it was too late to do any good.

The driver didn't say anything for a long time. He was thinking it over, and he was a slow thinker. Then finally he suggested offhandedly, "Care to listen to the radio?"

Paine knew what he was out for. He thought, "He wants to see if he can get anything on me over it."

"May as well," the driver urged. "It's thrown in with the fare; won't cost you nothing extra."

"Go ahead," Paine consented. He wanted to see if he could hear anything himself.

It made the pain a little easier to bear, like music always does. "I used to dance, too," Paine thought, listening to the tune, "before I started killing people."

It didn't come over for a long time.

"A city-wide alarm is out for Richard Paine. Paine, who was about to be dispossessed from his flat, shot and killed a finance company employee. Then when Officer Harold Carey answered the alarm, he met the same fate. However, before giving up his life in the performance of his duty, the patrolman succeeded in seriously wounding the desperado. A trail of blood left by the fugitive on the stairs leading up to the roof over which he made good his escape seems to confirm this. He's still at large but probably won't be for long. Watch out for this man—he's dangerous."

"Not if you leave him alone, let him get to that train," Paine thought ruefully. He eyed the suddenly rigid silhouette in front of him. "I'll have to do something about him—now—I guess."

It had come through at a bad time for the driver. Some of the main driveways through the park were heavily trafficked and pretty well lighted. He could have got help from another car. But it happened to come through while they were on a dark, lonely byway with not another machine in sight. Around the next turn the bypass rejoined one of the heavy-traffic arteries. You could hear the hum of traffic from where they were.

"Pull over here," Paine ordered. He'd had the gun out. He was only going to clip him with it, stun him and tie him up until after eight-twenty.

You could tell by the way the driver pulled his breath in short that he'd been wise to Paine ever since the news flash, had only been waiting until they got near one of the exits or got a red light. He braked. Then suddenly he bolted out, tried to duck into the underbrush.

Paine had to get him and get him fast, or he'd get word to the park division. They'd cork up the entrances on him. He knew he couldn't get out and go after him. He pointed low, tried to hit him in the foot or leg, just bring him down.

The driver had tripped over something, gone flat, a moment ahead of the trigger fall. The bullet must have ploughed into his back instead. He was inert when Paine got out to him, but still alive. Eyes open, as though his nerve centers had been paralyzed.

He could hardly stand up himself, but he managed to drag him over to the cab and somehow got him in. He took the cap and put it on his own head.

He could drive—or at least he'd been able to before he was dying. He got under the wheel and took the machine slowly on its way. The sound of the shot must have been lost out in the open, or else mistaken for a backfire; the stream of traffic was rolling obliviously by when he slipped into it unnoticed. He left it again at the earliest opportunity, turned off at the next dark, empty lane that offered itself.

He stopped once more, made his way to the back door, to see how the cabman was. He wanted to help him in some way if he could. Maybe leave him in front of a hospital.

It was too late. The driver's eyes were closed. He was already dead by this time.

Five.

It didn't have any meaning any more. After all, to the dying death is nothing. "I'll see you again in an hour or so," he said.

He got the driver's coat off him and shrouded him with it, to keep the pale gleam of his face from peering up through the gloom of the cab's interior, in case anyone got too close to the window. He was unequal to the task of getting him out again and leaving him behind in the park. The lights of some passing car might have picked him up too soon. And it seemed more fitting to let him rest in his own cab, anyway.

It was ten to eight now. He'd better start for the station. He might be held up by lights on the way, and the train only stopped a few minutes at the uptown station.

He had to rejoin the main stream of traffic to get out of the park. He hugged the outside of the driveway and trundled along. He went off the road several times. Not because he couldn't drive, but because his senses fogged. He pulled himself and the cab out of it each time. "Train, eight-twenty," he waved before his mind like a red lantern. But like a spendthrift he was using up years of his life in minutes, and pretty soon he was going to run short.

Once an alarm car passed him, shrieking by, taking a short cut through the park from one side of the city to the other. He wondered if they were after him. He didn't wonder very hard. Nothing mattered much any more. Only eight-twenty—train—

He kept folding up slowly over the wheel and each time it touched his chest, the machine would swerve crazily as though it felt the pain, too. Twice, three times, his fenders were grazed, and he heard faint voices swearing at him from another world, the world he was leaving behind. He wondered if they'd call him names like that if they knew he was dying.

Another thing: he couldn't maintain a steady flow of pressure on the accelerator. The pressure would die out each time, as when current is failing, and the machine would begin drifting to a stop. This happened just as he was leaving the park, crossing the big circular exit plaza. It was controlled by lights and he stalled on a green out in the middle. There was a cop in control on a platform. The cop shot the whistle out of his own mouth blowing it so hard at him. He nearly flung himself off the platform waving him on.

Paine just sat there, helpless.

The cop was coming over to him, raging like a lion. Paine wasn't afraid because of what the back of his cab held; he was long past that kind of fear. But if this cop did anything to keep him from that eight-twenty train—

He reached down finally, gripped his own leg by the ankle, lifted it an inch or two clear of the floor, let it fall back again, and the cab started. It was ludicrous. But then some of the aspects of death often are.

The cop let him go, only because to have detained him longer would have created a worse traffic snarl than there was already.

He was nearly there now. Just a straight run crosstown, then a short one north. It was good he remembered this, because he couldn't see the street signs any more. Sometimes the buildings seemed to lean over above him as though they were about to topple down on him. Sometimes he seemed to be climbing a steep hill, where he knew there wasn't any. But he knew that was just because he was swaying around in the driver's seat.

The same thing happened again a few blocks farther on, directly in front of a large, swank apartment house, just as the doorman came flying out blowing a whistle. He'd caught hold of Paine's rear door and swung it wide before the latter could stop him, even though the cab was still rolling. Two women in evening dress came hurrying out of the entrance behind him, one in advance of the other.

"No—taken," Paine kept trying to say. He was too weak to make his voice heard, or else they ignored it. And he couldn't push his foot down for a moment.

The foremost one shrieked, "Hurry, Mother. Donald'll

never forgive me. I promised him seven-thirty—"

She got one foot on the cab doorstep. Then she just stood there transfixed. She must have seen what was inside; it was better lighted here than in the park.

Paine tore the cab away from her, open door and all, left her standing there petrified, out in the middle of the street in her long white satin gown, staring after him. She was too stunned even to scream.

And then he got there at last. He got a momentary respite, too. Things cleared a little. Like the lights going up in a theater when the show is over, before the house darkens for the night.

The uptown station was built in under a viaduct that carried the overhead tracks across the city streets. He couldn't stop in front of it; no parking was allowed. And there were long lines of cabs on both sides of the no-parking zone. He turned the corner into the little dead-end alley that separated the viaduct from the adjoining buildings. There was a side entrance to the station looking out on it.

Four minutes. It was due in another four minutes. It had already left downtown, was on its way, hurtling somewhere between the two points. He thought, "I better get started. I may have a hard time making it." He wondered if he could stand up at all.

He just wanted to stay where he was and let eternity wash over him.

Two minutes. It was coming in overhead, he could hear it rumbling and ticking along the steel viaduct, then sighing to a long-drawn-out stop.

That sidewalk looked awfully wide, from the cab door to the station entrance. He brought up the last dregs of vitality in him, broke away from the cab, started out, zigzagging and going down lower at the knees every minute. The station door helped pull him up straight again. He got into the waiting room, and it was so big he knew he'd never be able to cross it. One minute left. So near and yet so far.

The starter was calling it already. "Montreal express—

eight-twenty!—Pittsfield, Burlington, Rouse's Point, Mon-
treyall! Bo-o-ard!"

There were rows of lengthwise benches at hand and they
helped him bridge the otherwise insuperable length of the
waiting room. He dropped into the outside seat in the first
row, pulled himself together a little, scrambled five seats
over, toppled into that; repeated the process until he was
within reach of the ticket barrier. But time was going, the
train was going, life was going fast.

Forty-five seconds left. The last dilatory passengers had
already gone up. There were two ways of getting up, a long
flight of stairs and an escalator.

He wavered toward the escalator, made it. He wouldn't
have been able to get by the ticket-taker but for his hack-
man's cap—an eventuality he and Pauline hadn't foreseen.

"Just meeting a party," he mumbled almost unintelligibly,
and the slow treadmill started to carry him up.

A whistle blew upstairs on the track platform. Axles and
wheel-bases gave a preliminary creak of motion.

It was all he could do to keep his feet even on the escalator. There wasn't anyone in back of him, and if he once
went over he was going to go plunging all the way down to
the bottom of the long chute. He dug his nails into the as-
cending hand-belts at both sides, hung on like grim life.

There was a hubbub starting up outside on the street
somewhere. He could hear a cop's whistle blowing fren-
ziedly.

A voice shouted: "Which way'd he go?"

Another answered: "I seen him go in the station."

They'd at last found what was in the cab.

A moment after the descending waiting-room ceiling had
cut off his view, he heard a spate of running feet come surg-
ing in down there from all directions. But he had no time to
think of that now. He was out on the open platform upstairs
at last. Cars were skimming silkily by. A vestibule door was
coming, with a conductor just lifting himself into it. Paine
went toward it, body low, one arm straight out like in a fas-

cist salute.

He gave a wordless cry. The conductor turned, saw him. There was a tug, and he was suddenly sprawled inside on the vestibule floor. The conductor gave him a scathing look, pulled the folding steps in after him, slammed the door.

Too late, a cop, a couple of redcaps, a couple of taxi drivers, came spilling out of the escalator shed. He could hear them yelling a car-length back. The trainmen back there wouldn't open the doors. Suddenly the long, lighted platform snuffed out and the station was gone.

They probably didn't think they'd lost him, but they had. Sure, they'd phone ahead, they'd stop the train to have him taken off at Harmon, where it changed from electricity to coal power. But they wouldn't get him. He wouldn't be on it. Just his body.

Each man knows when he's going to die; he knew he wouldn't even live for five minutes.

He went staggering down a long, brightly lighted aisle. He could hardly see their faces any more. But she'd know him; it'd be all right. The aisle ended, and he had to cross another vestibule. He fell down on his knees, for lack of seat backs to support himself by.

He squirmed up again somehow, got into the next car.

Another long, lighted aisle, miles of it.

He was nearly at the end; he could see another vestibule coming. Or maybe that was the door to eternity. Suddenly, from the last seat of all, a hand darted out and claimed him, and there was Pauline's face looking anxiously up at him. He twisted like a wrung-out dishcloth and dropped into the empty outside seat beside her.

"You were going to pass right by," she whispered.

"I couldn't see you clearly, the lights are flickering so."

She looked up at them in surprise, as though for her they were steady.

"I kept my word," he breathed. "I made the train. But oh, I'm tired—and now I'm going to sleep." He started to slip over sidewise toward her. His head dropped onto her lap.

She had been holding her handbag on it, and his fall displaced it. It dropped to the floor, opened, and everything in it spilled out around her feet.

His glazing eyes opened for one last time and centered feebly on the little packet of bills, with a rubber band around them, that had rolled out with everything else.

"Pauline, all that money—where'd you get that much? I only gave you enough to buy the train tickets—"

"Burroughs gave it to me. It's the two hundred and fifty we were talking about for so long. I knew in the end you'd never go near him and ask for it, so I went to him myself— last night right after you left the house. He handed it over willingly, without a word. I tried to tell you that this morning, but you wouldn't let me mention his name. . . ."

Made in the USA
Las Vegas, NV
07 September 2023

77215879R00108